No Answers

It was so quiet that all I could hear was the sound of his deep, even breathing. I sighed. Must be nice to be able to do that. Turn off the world and go to sleep no matter how messed up things are. I wished I could do it, but I lay there all tensed up with a million questions running through my mind. Just questions. No answers.

**Other Point paperbacks
you will enjoy:**

Up Country
by Alden Carter

Probably Still Nick Swanson
by Virginia Euwer Wolff

Life Without Friends
by Ellen Emerson White

A Band of Angels
by Julian Thompson

DARE

Marilyn Halvorson

SCHOLASTIC INC.
New York Toronto London Auckland Sydney

ISBN 0-590-43545-0

12 11 10 9 8 7 6 5 4 3 2 1   2 3 4 5 6 7/9
Printed in the U.S.A.   01
First Scholastic printing, June 1992

To Marilyn and Ken
For being what friends are all about

Thanks to everyone who shared the knowledge
and experience that made the story work.
And special thanks to Nicola for the idea
behind it all.

Chapter 1

We'd been hanging out in the Three G's Café for nearly an hour now, ever since the movie let out. There were five of us; me, Keith Ericsson, a couple of girls and, of course, Ty, my kid brother. It wasn't exactly what I'd call exciting, drinking Cokes and killing time, but in a town like Crossing, that's about as exciting as it gets — especially when you're not old enough to have a driver's license. I wasn't old enough, that is. Keith was, but he drove his motorbike through his mom's sweet peas last week and she confiscated his keys.

I looked at my watch. Nearly eleven. Gran was going to rag at us for being out so late on a school night but I didn't care. My marks couldn't get much worse, and Ty's were too good for a little lost sleep to mess them up.

Bored out of my mind, I looked around for something to do — and found the answer staring right back at me. I looked at Keith. "Bet you I can hit him right between the eyes," I said lazily, sizing up the enemy.

Keith shook his head. "No way, Dare," he said, his voice scornful. "You'll never do it."

"Oh, yeah?" I said, instantly accepting the challenge. I've never passed up a dare in my life, which is half the reason for my nickname. "Why don't you put some money on it if you're so sure, Ericsson?"

"You got it, man." Keith dug in his pocket and came up with two quarters. "Fifty cents says you can't."

I matched him with one quarter, two dimes, two pennies and . . . "Hey, Ty, you got three cents?" I asked. Silently, he pulled out a handful of change and sorted out the pennies. As kid brothers go, I could have done worse, even if he does always hang around with me.

I laid the change on the table. "Fifty cents says I can."

"Okay, go for it," Keith said, eyeing the victim.

Concentrating hard, I sucked up a straw full of Coke. I held my breath, took careful aim and fired! But the moth-eaten moose head never even blinked. It just kept staring mournfully from the café wall as a trail of Coke began to slide down that wall from a spot just above its left ear.

Well, there went my fifty cents and . . .

"Dare!" The waitress let out an ear-splitting yell that made me jump. "You pull that again and you're out of here, all of you."

I leaned back in my chair and gave her a lazy smile. I knew her pretty well. She was just a couple of grades ahead of me in school. "Sorry, Deb," I said innocently. "I didn't mean to do that." It was the truth. I hadn't meant to hit the wall. I'd meant to hit the moose.

"Sure you didn't," she said, wiping the Coke off the wall. But there was a hint of a smile at the corners of her mouth, and I knew she was going to forgive me. I get along pretty good with girls — when I want to. But right about then I noticed the look that Sue Kiniski, my sort-of date, was giving me. It was cold enough to cause goose pimples. Obviously I wasn't getting along with her right now.

I guess she figured that I wasn't allowed to smile at another girl while I was with her. That burned me some. Sit with her in the movie — I hadn't even paid her way in — and she thinks she owns me. Well, she could think again. She didn't own me. Nobody owned me.

"Pay up, sucker," Keith said with a mocking grin.

Grudgingly, I dropped my change into his outstretched hand. "Just a fluke, man," I said. "That was a defective straw. Next time . . ." But I never finished the sentence because just then something outside the window caught my eye. A police car, pulling into the parking lot. Cop cars always make me nervous, even when I haven't done anything. I guess everyone else noticed the car, too, because a sudden silence fell over the table.

We watched as the door of the car opened and Corporal Steiger got out — the guy at the top of my list of people I wouldn't want to get stranded on a desert island with. Deliberately, I reached over and took one of Keith's cigarettes from the package on the table. I hardly ever smoke, but since that time Steiger saw me smoking at the arena a couple of years ago and made a federal case about how he hates to see kids smoking, I make it a point to rattle his chain whenever I get the chance.

Steiger walked into the café. He stood a minute, looking around. Then his cold gaze came to rest on me. He started walking toward our table — and I started thinking fast. Trying to remember what I'd done lately that was serious enough to rate as cop business. My mind came up a complete blank. Halloween was seven months ago — and I hadn't done anything that wouldn't wash off, anyhow. There was that business at school today, I thought, feeling the letter lying stiff and accusing in my shirt pocket. No, that couldn't be it. They don't throw you in jail for lipping off teachers, not even in Crossing, Alberta.

I was out of time for thinking. Steiger was standing by my chair, giving me his Clint Eastwood stare. "Darren Jamieson?" he said in his all-business voice, and I almost burst out laughing. He was really getting his kicks playing policeman tonight. I mean, I've lived in this town since I was eight years old, and Steiger and I had been through enough run-ins that he didn't need to check my identity now. Half a dozen smart remarks flashed through my mind right then but I didn't say any of them out loud. I just returned Steiger's cold stare.

He jerked his head over his shoulder. "Darren

Jamieson, come over here," he ordered. "I'd like to talk to you alone for a minute."

Four sets of eyeballs drilled holes in me as I stood up — real slow and cool-looking, I hoped — and followed the cop over to a corner of the room.

A minute later I was back at the table. "Come on, Ty," I said, throwing my last two bucks on the table and picking up my jacket. Ty didn't ask questions. Nobody at the table did. They all just sat there staring as Tyler and I followed Steiger outside and climbed into the back of the police car.

Steiger screeched his tires a little and pulled out onto the main street. I glanced over at Ty. His eyes were like saucers. I knew this was the first time he'd been in a police car. I couldn't decide which he was, awestruck at the honor or terrified that he was on a nonstop trip straight to the slammer. Well, it wasn't my first time and I didn't feel either honored or terrified. All I felt right now was kind of sick.

"Dare?" Ty's voice was hushed, as if he figured they'd add a year to his sentence just for opening his mouth, but there was nothing subdued about the way he was digging me in the ribs with his elbow. He wanted some answers — now.

"Gran had a stroke," I said, keeping my voice real low. I don't know why I thought it would help to whisper. Maybe it just seemed like saying it out loud would make it too real.

Ty didn't say anything for a minute. He's always been like that. When something hits him hard he gets real quiet while he sorts it out in his head.

Finally he turned to look at me. Even in the dim glow of the passing streetlights, I could feel those serious eyes boring into me, demanding the truth. "She's gonna be all right, though, isn't she, Dare?"

I sighed. The kid had been doing this to me all his life, expecting me to come up with all the answers. "I don't know, Ty," I said wearily. "He's takin' us to the hospital to find out."

Steiger wheeled into the hospital parking lot and cut the engine. We waited while he got out and came and jerked the back door open. Then he stood there beside it, all straight and tall like he was the gestapo or something.

I didn't even look at him as we climbed out and started walking toward the hospital door. He fell into stride beside me. "Your grandmother was a good woman," he said, like that piece of information was a real surprise to me.

Was? I thought. What did he mean *was?*

"Too bad you never learned to appreciate her," he went on. "If you had, maybe she wouldn't have been home alone when it happened. Who knows how long she was lying there helpless."

Sure, rub the guilt in a little deeper.

"Who knows how much longer it would have been if Mrs. Henry down the street hadn't just happened to drop in? It could have been a long time if she'd been counting on you."

Angrily, I turned to look at him. "We would have been home in another hour," I said, mad at myself for giving him the satisfaction of any answer. Then, before he could say anymore, I turned away and broke into a run. Ty was keeping pace right beside me but I was relieved to see that Steiger just kept walking. Running probably didn't fit the "cool-cop" image he had of himself. I was just glad to get away from him. Walking into the hospital with a police escort was more than I could handle right now. I'd had to do it once before and it wasn't an experience I wanted to repeat.

As a matter of fact, I thought as we walked through the front doors, I hadn't been here since that time. Hospitals are places I stay away from unless I'm half dead — well, even if I am half dead, I guess. I sure hadn't wanted to come here the day I tried to prove it was possible to ride a motorcycle up the steep side of Kagan's Butte.

Just for the record, it wasn't possible. I came close. Real close. I was almost to the top before the bike flipped. I came out of it okay, though. Well, not as okay as I would have been if the bike hadn't landed on top of me. But I *was* on my feet when the cop car came howling up to the scene of the accident — or crime, the way Steiger had acted. By the time he'd finished yelling at me about hazardous stunts, I was starting to feel kind of funny and all I wanted to do was go home and lie down for a while. But of course Steiger couldn't let it go at that. He had to drag me to the hospital. They found out I had two cracked ribs and a concussion and I ended up stuck in this place for three days.

But as that scary hospital quiet settled in around

us, I realized that I hadn't felt as bad that day as I did right now. Then, I knew I'd heal. Everything would be back to normal in a little while. But this time I wasn't so sure the empty feeling in the pit of my stomach would ever go away.

Chapter 2

Awkwardly, I edged up to the desk and stood waiting for somebody to notice me standing there. Finally a nurse looked up. "Yes?" she said, giving me a sour look like she didn't think I belonged there.

"We're here to see, uh . . ." I hesitated. For one crazy second I couldn't even think of her name. She was never anything but Gran to us. "To see Ann Hilton," I finished, feeling my face start to burn.

The nurse's expression got even more disapproving. "That's not possible, I'm afraid. She's in intensive care and not allowed visitors. Perhaps if you were to come back tomorrow . . ." She let the sentence die and turned back to her stack of papers like we were a problem she had just solved.

I felt the short cord on my temper starting to fray. "Look, lady," I said loud enough to get her attention, "we just got dragged down here in a cop car to see our grandmother and now you're tellin' us that — "

"Young man — " she cut me off with a voice that snapped like a spring trap " — I am telling you — "

Right then a man in a white coat came around the corner, walking fast like he was going somewhere. That got the nurse's attention. "Oh, Dr. Musiak," she called, "this young *gentleman* — " the way she said the word, it didn't sound like a compliment " — is inquiring about Mrs. Hilton."

The doctor came to the desk. "You're her grandson then, I assume?"

I nodded. "Yeah, me and Ty both." Ty was right beside me, sticking to me as close and quiet as a shadow.

Dr. Musiak glanced at him and then looked back at me. "I think you'd better come with me for a moment," he said quietly. Then he gave Ty a reassuring smile. "Just wait in the lounge for a few minutes, son. I think you'll find a pretty good selection of comic books in there."

Ty shot me a look so full of rebellion that I couldn't help smiling. The doctor didn't exactly understand the situation. My brother was twelve, looked ten and acted forty most of the time. If Dr. Musiak had known us he probably would have sent *me* to read comics and taken Ty for a man-to-man talk. But he didn't know us. I returned Ty's look. "Just do it," I said quietly. "I'll be right back." He turned away reluctantly and I followed the doctor into an office.

He shut the door, sat down and motioned me to the other chair. I stayed standing. I just wanted to get this over with and get out of there. "So," I said, my voice sounding cool, "is she gonna be okay?"

He gave me another long look. I guess he decided I was old enough to level with because he shook his head. "I'm afraid not," he said gently, and then he paused, waiting for some reaction from me. I don't know what he expected I was going to do. Cry? I didn't do anything and finally he started talking again.

"Your grandmother has had a very severe stroke," he said, "and at her age and considering the amount of neurological damage, it is unlikely that she will regain consciousness." I waited for him to finish that sentence. Unlikely that she will regain consciousness for a week? For a month? For a long time? Then, suddenly, it hit me. The sentence was finished. He was talking *forever*.

"You mean she's as good as dead?"

The doctor gave me a real strange look and what he said next really blew me away. "You know, son," he said, his voice real soft, "when something like this happens it's all right to admit that it hurts. It's a human reaction. We all — "

Anger swept through me. What'd this guy think, he was a shrink or something? "Hey," I said, cutting him off, "I asked a simple question. All I need is an answer, not a sermon."

He breathed a deep sigh. "Let's just say her chances don't look good. In the morning we'll reassess her condition and possibly move her to Calgary, where they have better facilities." He took off his glasses and rubbed his eyes. "They may be able to prolong her life for a few days, weeks maybe, but . . ." He let the rest of the sentence trail off but I got the message. From here on, it was going to be just me and Ty.

"Can we see her?" I asked, and then wondered why I'd asked. I knew it was a real rotten way to feel, but deep down, I didn't want to see her.

He shook his head. "No, not in her present condition. She wouldn't even know you were there. The best thing I can suggest for you boys to do right now is go home and get some sleep. Give yourself a chance to get things in perspective." He gave me that searching look of his again and I knew he was still thinking that I was real tore up inside and just putting on this cool act to prove how macho I was or something. He just couldn't seem to get it through his head that I wasn't feeling much of anything at all.

We walked back to the waiting room. Ty saw us coming and put down the magazine he'd been reading. It wasn't a comic. It was *TIME* magazine.

"Dare, how is she?" he asked, standing up.

Dr. Musiak didn't give me a chance to answer. Probably afraid of what I'd say. "Your grandmother's pretty sick, son," he said, gently, "but she's sleeping comfortably right now and we don't want to disturb her."

Aw, come on, Doc. Give the kid a break. You think the truth's gonna be any easier for him to take when she's dead? What're you tryin' to do? Save it for a surprise? But he just kept on talking.

"You two had better just go home for the night

and . . ." He stopped and looked thoughtful. "Is there someone to look after you there?" I guess it had just occurred to him that if we were the closest relatives, that didn't leave any other adults around.

"I can take care of us," I said, but right away I knew that was a mistake. Next thing he'd be checking into how old I was and from there we'd get turned over to Social Services.

I lie pretty good when I'm put to it and, considering the amount of trouble I get myself into, I seem to be put to it fairly often. This looked like one of those times. "And," I added real fast, "our Aunt Ruth from Edmonton will be down tomorrow to look after things."

I heard Ty take a sudden breath and I knew he was getting ready to open his mouth and blow my great cover story all to pieces. I shifted my weight just enough to give him a dig in the ribs with my elbow. He jumped and gave me a startled look, but he got the message. He kept his mouth shut.

I took a quick glance around the lobby. Corporal Steiger wasn't hanging around anyway. If we could just ditch the doctor, we were home free. "Uh, thanks for everything," I said, amazing myself at my own politeness. "We'd better get home so we can get up in the morning to meet Aunt Ruth. Let's go, Ty," I said, edging toward the door.

Without a word, Ty followed. My brother may be a little on the over-innocent side, but at least you don't have to draw him pictures.

We stepped out into the night — and into a cold

Alberta rain. I turned up my collar. The mile and a half home was going to be a long, wet walk. Still, it felt better out here than in there. I started walking fast. In spite of being about six inches shorter, Ty stayed right beside me. I knew what was on his mind. Sure enough: "Dare," he said, his voice accusing, "we don't have an Aunt Ruth."

"No kiddin'."

"But you told — "

I sighed and stopped walking. I'd been wrong. I *did* have to draw him pictures. "Ty," I said, wearily, "how do you manage to get on the honor roll at school?"

He looked up at me, his blond hair and wet face shining in the glow of a streetlight. Sometimes when he looks at me with his head at that certain angle he looks so much like the way I remembered Mom.

"What's being on the honor roll got to do with Aunt Ruth?" he asked, sounding puzzled.

I started walking again, but slow, at talking speed. We were going to be soaked by the time we got home anyway. "We've got an Aunt Ruth," I explained patiently, "because if we don't have one we're gonna end up back in another foster home. Is that what you want?"

Tyler's eyes widened. "No," he said in a strange voice and I wondered how much of that time eight years ago he could remember. Not much, I hoped. He'd only been four then. And I'd been seven.

Suddenly, I wished I hadn't got him started

thinking about it. I wished I hadn't got *me* thinking about it.

When we were only a couple of blocks from home, I said, "Hey, race you to the house."

Ty flashed the first grin I'd seen him come up with all night. "You're on!" he said, and he was gone. I took off after him but I knew I didn't stand a chance. Running was serious stuff to Ty. He was on the track team and he trained hard. Besides, he was about thirty pounds lighter than me.

He was already fishing the spare house key out of the flowerpot on the porch when I came panting up the steps. He grinned at me. "Oughta try a little clean livin', Dare."

"And take all the fun outa life? No way. Besides, who wants to be the world's fastest human, anyhow?"

"I do," he said, and I figured he probably meant it.

Chapter 3

He unlocked the door and we went in the house. It was real quiet in there. Weird quiet. Any other time if we came in late like this, Gran would be in bed and the house would be dead silent. But it wouldn't be like it was now. Because then we'd know she was there and that made things a whole lot different. I just stood there for a minute, not doing anything, not even really thinking anything. It was like I was waiting for somebody to tell me what to do next. I almost laughed when that thought hit me. Me wanting anybody to tell me anything had to be a first.

I took off my wet jacket and threw it in the general direction of a kitchen chair. It missed and landed in a soggy heap on the floor. Right away, Tyler was on my case about it.

"Hey, come on, Dare, can't you even hang it up? Gran works hard to keep that floor clean." Angrily he stalked over, picked it up and hung it on the bathroom door.

It was nothing. I should have just let it go but

right then my nerves were stretched pretty thin. "Knock it off, Ty. I got enough to worry about without you startin' to rag at me. The kitchen floor ain't gonna make much difference to Gran now, anyhow." As usual, the words were out before I stopped to think but the second I said them I regretted it. Ty was just standing there in the middle of the room, shivering, his own wet jacket still on, the water dripping from his hair into his eyes, staring at me like I'd announced the end of the world.

I forced a grin and changed the subject fast. "Hey," I said, "take off that wet coat or you're gonna get pneumonia or something."

He acted like he hadn't even heard me. He didn't move, and those level, smoke-colored eyes of his never left my face. "Is she gonna die, Dare?" he asked at last, his voice quiet but demanding. I took a deep breath.

"How am I supposed to know?" I said, my voice going hard-edged and angry on me again. I might have said a lot more but I caught myself. One thing Ty didn't need was to be yelled at. In their own way Gran and he had been pretty close. A lot closer than she and I had been. But then he'd only been five when we came to live here so I guess she was the only mother he could really remember. But I'd been old enough that I could remember — way too much.

I jerked my mind away from the past. There was nothing back there I wanted to think about. I went in the bathroom, grabbed a couple of towels and tossed one to Ty. "Hey," I said, "quit worryin'. Everything's gonna work out okay."

He caught the towel and seemed to lighten up a little. "You really think so, Dare?"

"Sure," I said with a grin.

It took a while to get dried off. Even then, we were still shivering. Gran would have made hot chocolate, I thought, so I looked in the cupboard for the hot-chocolate powder. There was only about a teaspoon left in the can. So much for that idea. I put the coffeepot on instead. Mom and I used to drink coffee together when I was real little. I like the stuff but I can never remember how many scoops for how many cups. I shoveled in lots to be sure it was strong enough, let it boil for a while and poured out a couple of mugs. I handed one to Ty. He sniffed it suspiciously. "Go ahead and drink it," I said, "it's guaranteed to put hair on your chest." Ty rolled his eyes, took a sip and almost choked to death.

"That coffee," he managed to get out between coughs, "would put hair on the palms of your hands." He gave me a dirty look and dumped the rest down the sink. I just laughed and drank mine. I didn't see anything wrong with it.

By the time we got all that over with the kitchen clock was reading almost one-thirty. I'm about three-quarters owl anyway so time doesn't usually worry me much, but after everything that had happened tonight even I was ready to hit the sack.

Ty was already in bed when I came into the room,

but he wasn't asleep. I might have known he'd be reading. He always is. I glanced at the book. It was built about like a dictionary. *Dune*, it said on the cover. I remembered seeing the movie. Heavy-duty sci-fi. I didn't even understand half of what was happening on the screen and I sure didn't understand how anybody could actually *read* that stuff. But why knock it? The more books Ty read, the more book reports he could do for me.

I peeled off my clothes and climbed into bed. Then I reached over and switched off the lamp between the beds. "Hey, Dare," Ty howled, "turn that back on. I'm at this real gross part — "

"The whole thing looks gross to me. Besides, tomorrow's a school day and we've gotta get up in the morning."

"*You're* tellin' *me* that? Who always has to wake who up in the morning, huh, Dare?"

I ignored that comment. Talking about school had reminded me of something. I turned the light back on but not for Ty. I got up and picked up my shirt, hoping that maybe I'd imagined that letter in the pocket and that by now it might have just disappeared.

It hadn't. So I dragged it out. It was addressed to Mrs. Ann Hilton, but I'd torn it open as soon as I got it out of the office. There's no way I'm about to hand over a letter from the principal that I haven't read — especially when I know I'm the main character in it. I could have predicted what it said, anyway. I've had more of those letters than I can count in the past few years, and they're all the same. Darren's attitude is unsatisfactory. Darren does not apply himself to his schoolwork. Darren's behavior at school is unacceptable. Yeah, and school is unacceptable to Darren, too.

This letter was just like all the others. But there was one catch. This time Darren was not going to be allowed back into class unless this letter was signed by his guardian to prove that she'd actually read it and understood how Darren was single-handedly destroying an otherwise perfect school. Considering the way things were, getting that signature was going to be a little bit tricky.

I sat there staring at the letter and feeling the anger build inside me. I hated that school. I hated everything about it. The bells that told you when you could come in, go home, sit down, stand up, eat lunch, go to the can. The teachers — all the wimps who couldn't make it in the real world facing people their own age — in there enjoying their little power trips breaking kids who didn't dare fight back. The principal who thought he was king, running his own little empire like he owned the whole place. Come to think of it, I even hated most of the kids.

Tyler interrupted my hate-a-thon. He had closed the book. "Come on, Dare," he said, yawning as he buried his head in the pillow. "You wanted to go to sleep so bad. Turn out the light."

"Just hang on a minute. There's something you gotta do for me."

"Yeah?" he said cautiously, sitting up and giving

me a look that was half curiosity and half suspicion. "What?"

I tossed the letter on his bed. "Sign this for me."

He picked up the envelope and looked at it. Then he looked at me. Slowly, he pulled out the letter and read it. Then he shook his head. "You really went and did it this time, didn't you, Dare?"

I glared at him. "I asked for a signature, not a lecture."

The glare didn't faze him any. Some people I can scare. Unfortunately, Ty isn't one of them. "So," he went on like he hadn't heard me, "which teacher did you lip off this time?"

"It was Phillips that sent me to the office," I muttered. "But I didn't do nothin'."

Ty laughed. "Save it, Dare. I've been around you too long to buy that line." Then his face went serious. "Why don't you just back off a little, Dare? It's just yourself you make it bad for. You can't beat the system."

I groaned. My own personal built-in guidance counselor. Just what I always wanted. "Ty," I said through my teeth, "just sign the paper, okay?"

He gave me a puzzled look. "What good's that gonna do?" he asked. "It's Gran's signature they want, not mine."

For being such a smart kid my brother could be awesomely vacant sometimes. "Right, Ty," I said. "You got it first try. So sign Gran's name."

Tyler's eyes widened. "You mean *forge* it?"

"I mean sign it so I can get into class tomorrow."

"But I can't — "

"Ty," I said, "if I don't show up with that paper signed, the principal's gonna phone Gran."

Ty was wide awake now. "And then what?" he asked in sort of a hushed voice.

"Guess," I said, feeling like everything that had happened today was suddenly catching up to me.

Ty didn't have to guess. He knew the answer as well as I did. "Social Services," he said.

I nodded. "That's when take over and start takin' care of us," I said bitterly. I figured we could take care of ourselves a lot better than some strangers in a foster home could take care of us, but I'd been around long enough to know that what I figured didn't matter a whole lot.

Ty sat up straight and pushed the hair out of his eyes. "Hand me the pen," he said.

The signature was close enough. I'd known it would be. Gran hadn't thought Ty's grade-three teacher knew much about handwriting so Gran had taught him herself the way she thought it should be. The result was that Ty wrote a whole lot like she did. Not exactly, but close enough to get by for now. And, deep down, I knew that "for now" was as long as we were going to get by with pretending nothing had changed anyway.

I put the letter in my pocket, climbed into bed and killed the light. "Thanks," I said, "you did a good job."

"Sure." Ty's voice came back wearily. "I did a

great job. You can mention that at my parole hearing when I go to jail for forgery."

I laughed. "Don't take it so hard, Ty. I'll come and visit you in the slammer. Now shut up and get some sleep, huh?"

"You're the one who's doin' all the talkin'," Ty shot back.

Maybe so, but I'd never known him to miss getting in the last word.

The sheets rustled as he settled down for the night and I rolled over and tried to do the same.

Chapter 4

I lay there in the dark, thinking. Mostly about Ty. He was growing up some. Getting smart with his big brother, I thought, grinning and wondering just how tough he really could be — if you scratched him deep enough to get through the gentleness.

It was so quiet that all I could hear was the sound of his deep, even breathing. I sighed. Must be nice to be able to do that. Turn off the world and go to sleep no matter how messed up things are. I wished I could do it, but I lay there all tensed up with a million questions running through my mind. Just questions. No answers.

All of a sudden the even breathing stopped. I heard Ty sit up again. "Dare," he said, wide awake, "what are we gonna do?"

"Everything's cool. We just keep good old Aunt Ruth around if anybody asks and go ahead and look after ourselves — "

Ty didn't let me finish. "I mean after," he said, and I heard him swallow. "If Gran really doesn't . . ." He broke off there but I didn't need to hear the rest of the sentence.

Good as I am at lying to other people, it never seems to work on Ty. I didn't even try this time. "I don't know," I admitted, jamming my pillow into a lump against the headboard and sitting up, too. It was going to be a long night.

I don't know what *we're* gonna do, I repeated silently. But I know what *I'd* do if it was just me. I'd be out of this place. Gone. Just hitch a ride to Calgary or maybe Vancouver. No. Not Vancouver. Not ever Vancouver again. How about California? Yeah. No more Alberta winters. Nothing but beaches and bikinis. I'd get by all right. I was big enough and tough enough. I'd survive — alone.

Ty broke into my thoughts again. "Maybe we could find Dad," he said softly.

He was always quiet when he talked about Dad, which wasn't very often. Sometimes I wondered how much he remembered about him. Ty had been only three when the old man took off. I was only six, as far as that goes, but I could remember a lot about him. He was the one I looked like — a big, dark guy with hard muscles and a bad temper, who came in yelling at night and went out yelling in the morning and who got his kicks knocking Mom and us kids around in between.

Outside of that, all I knew about him was that Mom had been crazy in love with him once. Crazy enough to run away with him when her mother had sworn she'd disown her if she did. But Mom was stubborn. She'd gone with him — and stuck with him for seven years. He was the one that took off in the end, to go work the rigs for big money in Egypt or somewhere, leaving her with us to raise alone. As far as I knew, he hadn't been back since.

"Don't count on it, Ty," I said. "If he was coming back he'd have been back before this."

"Okay then," Tyler said with a sigh, "you got any better ideas?"

There was a long silence. "Well, we're not gonna figure anything out tonight," I said at last. "Just trust me. I'll work something out. Now go to sleep, huh?"

Who was I tryin' to kid? We had two, maybe three days before somebody found out that poor old Aunt Ruth was no longer with us — and never had been. Then what? The foster-home scene again? You gonna let them do that to you again? I thought, grinding my fist into my pillow. No. Not the foster homes again. I'd run first. I'd done it before when I was a whole lot younger. And I'd do it again.

When Mom ran off with Dad she had burned her bridges behind her. Gran had said she never wanted to see her again and Mom was proud enough and stubborn enough to make sure she didn't. Nobody, not even us, knew we even had a grandmother. Since Dad was long gone, they put us in a foster home after Mom died. Homes was more like it. We went through seven in a year — and every time I ran, I took Ty with me. Some of them were bad, so

26

bad I don't even want to remember. A couple of them weren't so bad, though. In fact, one lady was real good to us. She reminded me a lot of Mom. I think that's why I had to get away from her. Some of the other places, I don't even know why I left. I just did.

Anyway, after the seventh place they decided they had to do something with us. Like maybe separate us and lock me up somewhere. But one social worker, this Mr. Wong, turned out to be kind of a special guy. Before he'd let that happen he went over all Mom's records one more time, found her birth certificate and managed to track down her mother. That's how we ended up with Gran.

"Hey." Ty's voice interrupted my thinking. "I bet Laura would help us."

"Laura!" I practically yelled the word into the peaceful darkness. "Don't you tell that nosy old bag anything about what's happening."

"Laura's not an old bag!" Ty shot back, just as loud and twice as angry. "You take that back."

Wow, there really *was* a temper under there somewhere. In about two seconds the world's first fistfight fought in complete darkness was about to take place.

"Okay, okay," I said, cooling down a little. "I know *you* like her. But you let her find out we're on our own here and she'll jump in with both feet just like she always does when she gets a chance to mind somebody else's business."

"You just don't like her because she's the only

teacher you can't bluff," Ty shot back, still sounding kind of mad.

That slowed me down for a minute. I wondered if there really might be some truth in it. Laura sure wasn't your average teacher. Actually she wasn't a regular teacher at all. She was just a substitute. When she wasn't teaching she was running a ranch a few miles out of town — by herself, too. I didn't know if she'd ever had a husband but she didn't have one now, anyway. Which wasn't surprising. She was too ornery for any man to live with.

She was too ornery for me to live with, too. I found that out last winter when Mr. Nowakowski, our language teacher, was away for a whole month, getting his gall bladder redecorated or something. And we got Laura McConnell. Ms. McConnell or Laura, she said to call her. In her opinion titles didn't have anything to do with respect, she said.

Well, most subs just take up a space and prevent major injuries and property damage. They don't actually try to teach you much. And if you've got a reputation as a troublemaker, they stay out of your way and hope you're not dangerous. Not Laura. She decided right away that I wasn't working up to my potential — that's one of her regular lines. I hardly ever work at all so she's probably right about that. But she got on my case about it. Detentions every time I didn't do my homework, extra study assignments if I failed a test. Sometimes I figured she had school all mixed up with her ranch and she had me pegged as some outlaw colt she was going to break or die trying.

But the clincher came on this big mid-term test she gave us. It was hard. Not multiple guess or anything like that. Just pages and pages of reading and writing. I finally got to the last question, a two-page essay. No way, José. I didn't write essays in the first place, and in the second place half the kids had already finished and gone home. So what if I failed? I'd failed before. I could do it again. I tossed the paper on her desk and headed for the door. But I didn't get there.

"Darren, you forgot something," Laura called out pleasantly. I turned around and went back — and got my test paper shoved in my face. "You forgot to finish this," she said in a voice that was low, but hard enough to cut glass. "Now sit down and don't get up until it's finished — properly." Her steel-gray eyes went through me like lasers.

I stared back. Nobody did this to me. But something in Laura's eyes told me she was one person who did. Glaring at her, I sat down — and sulked for half an hour. Then the bell rang. The last few keeners left and I stood up to go, too. Laura shook her head.

"Uh-uh, Dare. I said finish it. I meant finish it. There's no time limit on this test. I can wait."

The standoff lasted till four-thirty. That's when I gave up and started writing. One of the topics was freedom, and I suddenly had a lot to say on the subject. By five I was finished. I came out with the fourth-highest mark in the class.

That experience taught me two things — that I wasn't as dumb as I thought I was, and to stay away from Laura McConnell.

But with Ty and Laura it was a whole different ball game. They'd met when she was subbing for his grade-five teacher, and since Ty always *does* work up to his potential they'd got along fine, especially when Laura found out Ty was crazy over horses and would give anything for a chance to be a cowboy.

Laura gave him his chance. She started taking him out to her place and taught him to ride. He'd been spending nearly every other weekend out there since.

The more I thought about Ty and Laura the more I realized I wasn't being fair to Ty. I began to get an idea.

"Hey, Ty," I said slowly. No answer. "Ty?"

Rotten kid had gone to sleep on me.

Chapter 5

We were late for school the next morning. I don't even know why we bothered to go. But it never would have occurred to Ty to skip as long as he was alive and breathing, and I didn't know what else to do.

Classes had been started for about fifteen minutes when we finally walked into the front hall. As we passed the boys' can, the door suddenly opened and my old buddy Keith came out.

"Hey, man," he said, "I've been hangin' out in there all morning waiting for you. I was beginning to think Steiger had you locked up. What was all that about, anyhow?" There was nothing Keith enjoyed more than to see somebody get in trouble. Right now his nose was twitching like a hound's that had just caught wind of a possum.

I looked at him standing there with his naturally greasy hair greased up a little more into something he thought was cool, his two earrings, and that stupid grin on his face, and I realized I wasn't glad to see him. Even though he was a couple years older than me, we hung out together a lot and I guess people thought we were best friends. We weren't, though. Keith liked being around me because I got in plenty of trouble and had a reputation for being a tough kid. Keith liked to think he was a bad dude.

There were only two things about him I liked. One was that his parents were divorced and his mother was busy trying to be eighteen again. Her own social life didn't leave her much time for Keith, so he was the only kid in town who ran as wild as I did. The other thing — the most important thing — was Keith's bike, a big, bad, black Honda Shadow 500. His dad, who lived in Calgary now, had bought it for him when he turned sixteen. It was part of the war between him and Keith's mom. If he couldn't have custody, he was going to buy a little love. But I don't think it worked. As far as I could see, Keith didn't love anybody. He didn't even love the bike, not the way I did. I figured he was about half scared of it. Keith's kind of a scrawny little weasel, and the Shadow was just too much bike for him. It *was* about my size.

I shook my head and kept walking, wishing Keith would just go away. I didn't want to talk about last night. But he trailed along. I gave up. "It was nothin' to do with me," I said. "Gran had a stroke. Steiger took us to the hospital."

Keith's eyes widened. "No kiddin'? Geez, my old lady's aunt had a stroke and turned into a vegetable.

Everybody said it'd be better if she'd just croak 'cause it was only a matter of time anyway — "

I glanced at Ty. He looked like he was going to be sick. "Shut up, Ericsson," I muttered.

Keith gave me an insulted look. "Well, I was just — "

"Yeah," I said tiredly, starting to walk away again. "Come on, Ty. We gotta get late slips."

But Keith stopped me again. "Hey, what about the AC/DC tickets? You told me to get one for you. My old lady's pickin' 'em up in Calgary today. You ain't gonna back out, are you? I mean, what if your grandma — "

I shot him a warning look and this time he quit while he was still ahead. But not for long.

"I mean those things are twenty-five bucks apiece, man," he whined. "If I get stuck with yours — "

I cut him off. "Okay, okay, I get the message. I still want the ticket, all right?" Right about then that ticket was about number 999 on my list of problems, but anything to shut him up.

"Well, you don't have to get all choked about it. I was just askin'," he said, giving me a dirty look as he turned away.

Tyler and I walked on into the main office. Ty looked up at me. "I don't know what you see in that guy, Dare," he said, so serious that I couldn't help but grin at him.

"Me neither."

We sat on the bench and waited for the secretary,

Mrs. Batten, to look up from her typing and come see what we wanted. Getting late slips is one of those things about school that sure makes a lot of sense. You're late so you come down here and wait around until you're a whole lot later. That's about typical of how things work around this place.

Right about then the door to the teachers' workroom opened and I looked up — and almost swore out loud. Laura McConnell was the last person I needed to run into right now. And as soon as Laura realized it was me sitting there I could see the wheels start going around in her head. She glanced at the clock and I knew what she was thinking. She was going to start ragging at me for being late. But, just in time, Tyler spotted her.

"Laura!" he said, his eyes lighting up like he'd just won the lottery.

Laura's weathered face creased into a smile. "Hello, Tyler. Haven't seen you for a long time. Where you been the last few weekends?"

"I had a track meet last weekend. The one before was science fair. I was hoping I'd make it this weekend but . . ." He shot me a glance, caught my warning look and thought fast. "But I don't know if I'll have time," he finished. Before Laura had a chance to take that in, he changed the subject. "How's the sorrel filly comin'? You got her broke yet?"

"Chance? She's coming along real nice. I've been on her a few times. She's a little jumpy yet but there's not a mean bone in her. All she needs is work. That's why I've been hoping you'd come out and ride her for me. She's just turned two and I'm a little heavy for her."

Right then Mrs. Batten looked up, noticed us and came dozily mousing over to see what we wanted. But before she got there, the phone rang. She turned back and answered it, listened a minute and then for some reason looked over her shoulder at me. "Why, yes, I can get him right away," she said into the phone. "He's right here. One moment please."

She turned to me. "It's for you, Darren."

I just looked at her for a second. I didn't know anybody who would be phoning me at school. But as I walked over to the phone I got a sick feeling about who it might be — and why. I didn't think I wanted to hear this.

"Hello," I said reluctantly.

"Is this Darren Jamieson?"

"Yeah."

"Darren, this is Dr. Musiak." I'd guessed right. The doctor's voice went on. "I tried phoning your grandmother's home number. I thought your aunt would be there but I couldn't get her." There was a pause like maybe he thought I should say something. Under the circumstances, I didn't think I should say anything.

Dr. Musiak cleared his throat and hesitated like he was having trouble finding the right words. "Darren, your grandmother's condition has deteriorated seriously overnight. She is very critical but she has regained a degree of consciousness and has been asking for you and your brother. I think you should come as soon as possible. Can you get in touch with your aunt to bring you over?"

"No," I said. It was the first word that came to my mind and it was the answer to everything. But before he could say anything, I added, "We'll get there," and hung up.

My eyes met Tyler's. From the look on his face I knew he'd figured out what the call had been about. "Is she — " he began, but he almost choked on the words.

I shook my head. "She wants to see us," I said. "Let's go." I started toward the door but I never made it.

"What's wrong, Tyler?" Laura's voice cut in, a lot more gentle than I'd ever heard it.

Ty hesitated. He threw me a look that was half defiance, half apology. Then he looked at Laura. "Gran had a stroke," he said, just above a whisper. "She's real sick and she wants to see Dare and me."

Right then Laura took command. "Come on," she said, putting her arm around Ty's shoulders. "I'll drive you to the hospital." She turned to me then but, before she could say anything, Mrs. Batten interrupted.

"If you're leaving you'll need early-dismissal slips as well as late slips," she said, waving two pieces of paper and sounding like the future of the world depended on getting them filled out.

That did it. My whole life was messed up and she wanted me to fill out a form. I turned on her, furious. "You can take your early-dismissal slips and — " I never got finished. All of a sudden Laura's big, work-hardened hand was on my shoulder, squeezing hard.

"Let's go, Dare," she said through her teeth, practically pushing me out the door. "Never mind the paperwork, Margaret, I'll take responsibility for these two."

Chapter 6

Next thing I knew we were in Laura's truck. See, Ty, I thought, what'd I tell you? Just like that she takes control and we never knew what hit us.

Five minutes later we drove into the hospital parking lot. I opened the door, got out and waited for Ty to get out. I was even going to force myself to say thanks for the ride. But then, instead of driving away, Laura got out. I couldn't believe it as she started walking briskly toward the door with Ty beside her. Now she was going *in* with us. This was as bad as last night with Steiger. I walked in two paces behind, acting like I didn't know her.

But by the time we got to the desk I was secretly kind of glad Laura was there. This time *she* did the talking to the desk nurse, and she was a lot better at it than I was. A minute later a nurse was leading us down the hall to a door labeled "Intensive Care."

"Wait here, please," the nurse said and disappeared inside.

Yeah, I'd wait. I'd wait forever. I didn't want to

go in there. I didn't know how to act around sick people. I didn't know what to say to Gran. I didn't want to see her.

I looked at Laura talking quietly to Ty and for one short minute I was almost grateful to her. She really was good for him. Even I could see that. Just as long as she stayed away from me.

The door opened and Dr. Musiak came out. "Okay, boys," he said quietly. "You can see her now. One at a time. And only for a minute, she's very weak." He leaned over to talk to Ty. "You're Tyler?" he asked. Ty nodded. I felt a lump swelling up in my throat as I watched him. I knew how hard he was taking this but he was handling it with a lot of guts.

"She wants to see you first," the doctor said gently, opening the door for him. Then he nodded to Laura. "You'd better go with him," he said.

Laura followed.

I stood out in the hall alone, with about a hundred different thoughts running through my head. And none of them were very pretty. She wanted to see Ty first, I thought. Yeah, that figured. With Gran, Ty had always been first. I didn't really blame her. If I'd have been her I'd have liked Ty better, too. She treated me better than I deserved, considering how much trouble I caused. But still, there was always something between us, like a wall.

And Laura, just walking in there like she was family or something. And Ty acting the same way. What made Laura so special all of a sudden? Why wasn't I the one in there with him? I was his brother.

The door opened and Ty and Laura came out. Ty's face was wet but he wasn't crying now. Not quite. "She wants to see you, Dare," he said in a choked voice.

I took a deep breath and walked into the room. At first, I didn't even recognize Gran. I stared at this pale straggly-haired stranger lying there in the middle of a maze of tubes and wires. I just stood there.

Dr. Musiak looked up from the dials of some machine he was adjusting. "Come on in, Darren," he said. "You'll have to come close to hear her."

Like a robot, I moved closer to the bed. This wasn't really me. This wasn't really happening.

The stranger on the bed turned her head a little. Weakly, she reached out her thin hand and touched my arm. I barely fought back an instinctive urge to back away. Don't, Gran. Don't try to get close to me now. It's too late.

But she was dying — and reaching out to me. What was I supposed to do? Her cold, clammy hand found mine and gave it a weak squeeze. I held my hand still, steady as a rock, but inside I shivered. She stared up at me — no, through me, her faded blue eyes vague and unfocused like she was seeing another place, another time.

"Kathy?" she whispered. I just stared at her, not understanding. Then it hit me. Kathy had been my mother's name.

Oh God, I can't handle this. Get me out of here. I stood there, frozen, my whole body so tense it ached. She started talking again. Her voice was so weak I could barely hear the words. A ghost talking to a ghost.

"Kathy, I was always so hard on you," she said, shaking her head slightly. "And you were so stubborn. So hard on yourself. If only we could have both backed down a little I might not have lost you. But it's too late, Kathy . . ." Her voice trailed away and a tear slid down her lined cheek.

Don't do this to me, Gran. Talk about anything, but not about Mom. I was sweating. I wanted out, but she was still holding on to my hand. She raised her head a little, stared blankly at me for a second, and then she seemed to focus in on me at last. "Dare," she said, sounding almost surprised. "I was talking to your mother. You're so much like her."

I shook my head. She was really losing it. Me, like Mom? Not even close. Ty was the one like Mom. Small and blond. Except for my eyes I was the spitting image of my old man.

Gran was talking again. "You both always tried too hard. Too proud. Too stubborn. Trying to grow up too fast." She kept rambling on, her voice getting weaker. I tried not to listen. But the words kept on coming through.

"I always blamed you, Dare. I couldn't help it. But I should have blamed myself. If I could have just forgiven." She seemed to get a little stronger. She raised her head, and her voice was firmer. "I don't blame you any more, Dare. And your mother doesn't, either. It's time to stop blaming yourself." Her eyes looked right into mine for a second and her grip strengthened on my hand. Then she lay back with a sigh and her hand went limp.

I glanced up at the little screen above the bed. Dr. Musiak was looking at it, too. The little blip wasn't bouncing any more.

"It's all over," Dr. Musiak said gently, turning to look at me. "Did you understand what she was trying to tell you?"

I looked at him. He seemed like he was a long way off. "No," I said and walked dry-eyed out the door.

I walked past Laura and Ty like they weren't even there. Laura reached out and touched my shoulder. "Dare?" she said quietly. "Are you — "

I jerked away from her. "Leave me alone, Laura!" I yelled.

I went over to the window at the end of the hall and stood there staring out, trying to think. Maybe trying not to think. I don't know. I was so mixed up. Stop blaming yourself, Gran had said. Sure, Gran. That's real easy. Time's up. Just turn off the guilt tap now.

Dr. Musiak came up behind me and laid his hand on my shoulder. I shook him off.

"It's okay, son," he said, gently. "Go ahead and cry."

"I'm not cryin'," I said fiercely, blinking back the tears.

"Okay," he said, "okay." Then he nodded toward Laura. "This is your aunt?"

I stared at him. "What aunt?" I blurted out and as soon as I said it I knew what I'd done. But the show was about over anyway. There was no way to get through a funeral without people finding out.

The thought of the funeral made me go hollow inside. No, I couldn't go through another funeral. I wouldn't go. Sorry, Gran. Nothing personal. It's just that I haven't ever got over the other one. Try to understand, Gran. Maybe you can forgive me now. But I can't. Another thought hit me. Ty. There was always Tyler to think about. He'd want to go. And he'd want me to go with him.

Dr. Musiak brought me back to the present. "I wondered about the aunt story," he said thoughtfully. "How old are you, Darren?"

"Fifteen," I said.

"And your brother?"

"Twelve."

"And there are no other relatives?"

I shook my head. After nine years, Dad didn't count anymore.

The doctor rubbed his forehead wearily. I figured he'd been up all night with Gran. And now he was stuck with one more problem to dispose of.

Laura stepped forward. "I could take them home with me for now," she said. "My name's Laura McConnell."

That got my attention. I swung around, a loud *no* already in my mind. But I stopped myself in time. Shut up, Dare. Step one is to get out of this place, fast. You start making waves and they'll have you sitting around here all day while they hunt up somebody from Social Services.

The doctor hesitated. "Well, I'm afraid that regulations state that in a case like this I have to inform Social Services before children can be turned over to anyone other than members of the immediate family."

So much for that theory, Dare, I thought, wondering if I should just cut and run right now.

"But," Dr. Musiak went on, his tired face lighting up, "Mr. Nicholson from Social Services was coming in to speak to a patient first thing this morning. I think he's still here. I'll have him paged and maybe we can deal with this right here. Just wait in the waiting room a minute, please."

Ty sat by Laura. I sat on the other side of the room, pretending to read a magazine. But before long Ty came over to me. "It was best, wasn't it, Dare?" he said, his voice hoarse.

I looked up at him. "What?"

"Gran," he said, swallowing. "She said it was okay, that she was real tired and didn't mind dying and not to feel bad for her. And then she said she loved me, and — " his voice cracked and he wiped his arm across his eyes " — and that was all." He took a couple of deep, shaky breaths and got his voice under control. "What'd she tell you, Dare?"

I looked across the small room, saw Laura's eyes

on me and looked back at Ty. "She said she loved me, too," I said.

Right then Dr. Musiak walked in with Nicholson from Social Services. Nicholson and I knew each other from way back. He was the one who had come to the house the two times they'd almost taken me away from Gran for running wild and getting into too much trouble. I wasn't glad to see him.

The doctor introduced Nicholson and Laura. Then he told me and Ty to wait while Laura and Nicholson went down to the office to talk. We waited a long time.

Finally I had to go to the bathroom. I'd seen one down the hall. "Be back in a minute," I told Ty.

I wandered down the hall, slow, my mind about a million miles away. I was just about to turn into the bathroom when I thought I heard Laura's voice. The door to the office where Dr. Musiak had talked to me last night was open a little ways. I stopped and listened. It was Laura and Nicholson in there, all right.

"He's really a great kid," I heard Laura say. "I'd be happy to have him and I think living out there would be good for him, too."

There was a pause and then Nicholson's voice. "Yes, that certainly sounds feasible. Now, what about Darren? If at all possible we try to keep siblings together."

There was a longer pause. Then Laura's voice, in a tone I couldn't pin down, sort of regretful and almost laughing at the same time. "Dare?" she said. "Dare's a different story."

I'd heard enough. Angrily I walked into the bathroom and slammed the door. Yea, Laura, Dare's a different story — and don't you ever forget it.

All the way back to the waiting room I tried to figure out what I was so mad about. But I never did.

A few minutes later, a nurse came and called Ty to come down to the office. Then they called me. When I went down, Ty and Laura were standing down the hall a ways, talking. I couldn't hear what they were saying but they both looked pretty happy. They should look happy, I thought bitterly. All their problems just got solved.

I walked in and slumped into the chair across from Nicholson. He tried the politeness and small talk first. I ignored it, giving him a cold stare and waiting for him to get to the point. Finally he did.

"Well, Darren, you know we have to make some living arrangements for you." I just looked at him. "Now, of course, normally we would try to match you and your brother with one of our standing list of available foster homes. However, in this case, since Ms. McConnell is a reputable person who is willing and able to take you both — "

"To take Ty, you mean," I interrupted, my voice coming out cold and hard.

Nicholson gave me a funny look. "No, I mean both of you."

That was a switch, I thought, after what I'd overheard a few minutes ago. I wondered how much extra they were paying her to get stuck with me.

I shook my head. "No way, not me: I'm not goin' to her place. You couldn't pay me enough to live with Laura."

Nicholson sighed. "Any particular reason?"

"Yeah," I said. "I don't like her."

Nicholson was getting mad. It was kind of fun to watch. He was one of these super-civilized guys who didn't believe in losing his temper, and this was putting kind of a strain on him.

He cleared his throat. "Quite frankly, Darren, with your past record of running away from foster homes and your more recent reputation as a trouble-maker at school and around town, you're a more likely candidate for a juvenile detention center than for any foster home."

He paused to let that sink in. It did. I'd come pretty close to the edge a few times but I'd never quite landed in one of those places yet. And I didn't want to. They locked you up there.

"So, uh, what I'm trying to tell you, Darren," he said, almost apologetically, like it was all his fault I was such a rotten kid, "is that you're about out of chances. You're very lucky that Ms. McConnell has agreed to even try. She's really putting herself out for you, you know."

I'd never heard anyone who wasn't a teacher talk so much to say so little. Besides, I'd had it up to here with what a great person Laura McConnell was anyway. "All right, I get the picture," I interrupted. "So pin a medal on her and forget the speech."

Nicholson took his glasses off. "Darren," he said, and his tone wasn't apologetic anymore. I figured I'd better back off before I *did* land in a detention center — or his fist landed in my face.

"Okay, okay, I didn't mean that," I said.

Nicholson didn't answer. He just rubbed his forehead and put his glasses back on. He probably wanted me to say I was sorry. But I wasn't. And I wouldn't.

"Can I go?" I asked.

Nicholson nodded — gratefully, I think.

Chapter 7

By the time we got out of the hospital it was noon. Nobody was very hungry but Laura took us to the drive-in and got us hamburgers anyway. Then we went by Gran's to pick up some of our stuff. Going there wasn't something I wanted to do. It was like going back into a chapter of life that had been closed forever.

Laura went into the kitchen and started taking stuff out of the refrigerator so it wouldn't go bad, and Tyler and I walked down the empty hall to our bedroom. Silently, we started packing clothes. Ty stopped and turned to look at me. "Told you Laura would help," he said.

I stopped packing. "Yeah," I said sarcastically.

"What's that supposed to mean?"

I threw a sweatshirt in my duffel bag. "Look Ty," I sighed, "if livin' at Laura's and playin' cowboys is what you want that's fine with me. But it's not what I want."

Ty flopped down on his stomach on his bed and lay there with his chin propped up on his hands, studying me. "What *do* you want, Dare?" he asked.

I sat down on the bed, absentmindedly tracing the pattern on the afghan Gran had made. "What do I want? I want out of this town. I want to go to the city. Where the action is. Where they don't roll up the sidewalks at nine o'clock. I want to forget I ever heard of Crossing." I stood up and paced restlessly around the room.

Ty was quiet for a while. "Okay," he said at last. "If that's what you want to do, do it. But I'm comin' with you."

I spun around to face him. "Oh, no, you're not. The street's no place for a little kid."

"I'm not a little kid!" The anger in Ty's voice matched mine. "I can look after myself."

"You guys about ready?" Laura's voice interrupted us and her footsteps sounded in the hall. That killed the conversation, but from the last defiant look Ty shot in my direction, I knew the subject wasn't closed.

"Aren't you supposed to be working at school today, Laura?" Ty asked as she wheeled the truck out into the street.

Laura shook her head. "Not today. I was just in using the school copier to make copies of some registration papers I have to send in on the colts."

Ty was quiet a minute. Then, "Laura," he said hesitantly, "could we go back to school for the afternoon?"

I shot him a startled glance and saw Laura do the same. I mean, he was upset and everything, but he'd have to be crazy to want to go to school.

"You sure that's what you want, Ty?"

Ty nodded. "Yeah, I'm sure. We've got a real important science test today. Gran helped me study for it before . . . before she got sick. I promised her I'd get a good mark on it." His voice broke and he choked back a sob.

Laura reached her arm around his shoulders and gave him a hug. "Okay," she said, gently. "If you're sure you can handle it."

"I can handle it."

He probably could, I thought. My kid brother did some pretty weird things, but I had to admire his guts.

Then Laura glanced over at me. "How about you, Dare? You want to go to school, too?"

I almost burst out laughing. Did *I* want to go to school? Come on, Laura. Get real. And then I thought about the alternative. Spend the afternoon with Laura? "Yeah," I said.

Laura dropped us off at school and said she'd pick us up at the end of the day.

First afternoon class was social studies. It went all right. Mr. Pendleton wrote notes on the board all period. I didn't copy them. But I kept quiet. Pendleton accepted the compromise.

Then came science class — and Miss Phillips, the teacher I'd tangled with yesterday. Okay Dare, I thought, play it cool. You don't need any more trouble today.

Phillips started in on me right away. "Where's

the letter I sent home to your grandmother?" she asked.

I took it out of my pocket and tossed it on her desk. She unfolded it and looked it over. "And what did your grandmother have to say about your behavior?"

"Nothin'," I said, looking her in the eye. She looked like she was going to make something of it but she didn't. Not right then.

We had to do experiments on evaporation rates or something. Phillips put everybody in groups and assigned each group a burner to work with. But I got my very own. She didn't trust me with a group.

Slowly, I picked up the pack of paper matches, tore one off, closed the cover and stood there looking at it. Remembering.

I don't know how long I just stood like that, but all of a sudden Phillips was standing there, giving me the evil eye. I looked back at her. She was young and good-looking — and trying way too hard to act like a teacher, whatever they're supposed to act like.

"Come on, Darren," she said sarcastically, "not even your combustible personality is going to light that match just by looking at it. You're way behind everyone else, as usual. Get your burner lit."

I gave her an arrogant stare. Same to you, lady, I thought. But I didn't say it. I didn't say anything. I didn't do anything. I knew that would drive her crazy. It did. I could see her face start to get red. "Darren," she said in this real crisp teacher voice, "you have exactly three seconds to light that match."

Oh, wow, this was scary stuff. Slowly, deliberately, I dropped the unlit match on the counter. "And if I don't?"

Phillips's face turned a shade redder. I wondered if she was wishing she hadn't backed herself into this corner. I was kind of wishing I hadn't. Back off, lady, I thought. Quit hassling me and I'll get to work. But either Phillips didn't read vibes very well or she really wanted a showdown.

"If you don't," she said in a cold voice, "I will send you to the principal again."

Nice going, Dare. Twice in two days. You really need this, don't you? Okay, so light your little fire and cook your little experiment and make the lady's day.

But even as I was thinking, my temper broke loose. I threw the pack of matches at her. "You want it lit so bad, you light it!" I yelled. I turned and stalked out of the room. But not before I saw Miss Phillips suddenly start to cry.

I didn't know where I was going. Just out of that school. I almost made it. My hand was on the front door when I heard the principal's voice. "Darren! Get back here!"

The long walk down the hall had cooled me down a little. I turned around and walked into the office. Mr. Segal didn't even wait to get me in his private office. He started right in on me.

"All right, Darren. *Now* what is going on with

you? Miss Phillips has just called the office, very upset. What did you do in her class?"

"Nothin'," I said, staring at the floor. It was pretty close to the truth, but he didn't like it.

"Did you take that note home last night?" he asked, changing the subject.

"Yeah."

"Did you get it signed?"

"Yeah."

"And what would your grandmother have to say if I phoned her right now and told her about your latest escapade?"

"Nothin'."

"Do you mean to tell me she doesn't care how you behave?"

I looked up. "I mean to tell you she's dead," I said, my voice going funny on me.

You could have heard a feather fall. Segal just stood there gulping like a beached fish. I sensed someone standing behind me and glanced over my shoulder.

"Go get in the truck, Darren," Laura said, her voice quiet but firm.

For once I didn't argue. As I walked out, Laura and Segal were going into his office.

It seemed like I sat in the truck for a long time. The bell rang. Kids poured out and got on buses. But my mind was so far away none of it registered. Not even the fight on the playground, at first. A couple of younger kids. One quite a bit smaller than the other. That one, the little blond kid, was losing.

The other guy was beating the heck out of him, I thought vaguely, still not really focusing in on anything but what had happened in class. The little kid looked familiar.

Suddenly, I bailed out of the truck. "Ty!" I bellowed, heading for the playground at a dead run. The crowd dissolved when they saw me coming. By the time I got there Ty was the only one left. He was kneeling in the dirt wiping his bleeding lip on his torn shirt sleeve.

"What do you think you're doin'?" I yelled at him, dragging him to his feet. I couldn't believe this. Ty had never been in a fight in his life — and his performance showed it.

Beat up or not, though, he wasn't taking anything from me. "What are *you* so mad about? Fighting's how you solve everything."

"Yeah," I said, examining his lip, "but there's a difference. I'm good at it."

He gave me a nasty look but he didn't say anything to that. We started walking toward the truck. "So what was that all about?" I demanded.

Ty studied his sneakers. "You don't want to know."

I stopped walking. "Yeah, I want to know."

Tyler sighed. "Okay," he said. "It was about you."

"Me?"

He nodded. "A bunch of kids from your class were talking on the way out of school. Somebody said you made Miss Phillips cry in class. Then Allan

Morton said you were a crazy, dangerous hood that should be locked up. So I hit him."

There was only one thing to say. "Thanks, Ty," I said, barely hiding a grin. We climbed in the truck.

A minute later Laura got in. She started to say something to me, took a glance at Ty and did a double take. She shook her head wearily. "You two have had quite a day," she said. "Anything I ought to know about, Ty?"

"No, ma'am," he said.

Chapter 8

We headed for home — for Laura's place, I mean. Nothing could have been farther from home as far as I was concerned. We were almost there, I guessed, when all of a sudden Laura slammed on the brakes so hard I almost left a lasting impression on the windshield.

"Son of a gun," she growled. "J.R. has got out with the heifers again."

It took a minute but I finally realized she was talking about a half-grown red and white bull that was happily eating grass with some other half-grown critters.

Laura opened her door and started to get out. "Come on, Tyler," she said grimly, "we'd better get the little devil back in the corral or there'll be a whole bunch of too-early surprises next spring, just like Little Red Corvette was this year."

I stared at the herd of cows. If their names were any indication, Laura's critters must have a real interesting social life.

She crawled through the fence, walked up to

poor, unsuspecting J.R. and gave him a swat on the rump. He looked up, his mouth full of clover. With one sad glance over his shoulder at all those beautiful young heifers, he obediently set off for home. Tough luck, guy. From the way his love life was going, she should have named him Romeo.

Ty had caught up and was walking on the other side of the bull by the time Laura finally remembered me.

"Well, don't just sit there, Dare. Take the truck home. My ice cream's melting," she yelled.

I drove on up the long lane for the first time and got kind of a surprise when I saw how nice it was. There was a big, middle-aged, one-story house set in a huge green yard, a freshly painted barn that looked older than Laura and a lot of neatly painted outbuildings. It wasn't the kind of ranch that spelled big money; more like the kind that spelled hard work.

I parked the truck beside an older truck near the barn, picked up the grocery bag and headed for the house.

I was about halfway there when I heard hoofbeats behind me. At least I thought they were hoofbeats. It sounded like a Shetland pony. Except for one thing. It started to bark. I took a fast glance over my shoulder and there was the biggest German shepherd in Alberta pounding up behind me and flashing a set of teeth that would have made Jaws proud.

I don't like German shepherds. The last shepherd

I'd got closely acquainted with lived at the cop station in town. It was two years ago at Halloween when Keith dared me to egg the police car. Unfortunately, the dog took it as a personal insult, and before I could get out of there, he'd taken a big bite out of me, high up on the back of my left leg. Like, I mean *real* high. It's always kind of bugged me to have a nine-stitch scar I couldn't even show off.

But it didn't bug me enough to want to try for a better one. I took off running for the house. The dog speeded up.

I took the steps two at a time and flung myself against the door, twisting the knob at the same time. But the knob didn't twist. The door was locked.

There I stood, plastered against the door, still holding Laura's groceries and waiting for that dog to sink her teeth into me. But instead, she sat down on the ground by the bottom step, cocked her head sideways and studied me with puzzled concentration. Probably trying to decide where the best steaks are on a human, I thought grimly, staring at her open-mouthed grin.

It was Ty who showed up first. I could hear Laura hammering away at the fence on the other side of the barn as he came strolling over to the house. He stopped and stood there with his head cocked sideways like the dog's, gawking at me. "Dare," he said, interestedly, "what are you doin'?"

We studied the word "fratricide" in vocabulary

once. It means killing your brother, and I figured I'd finally found a use for it. "I'm standin' here tryin' not to get eaten while you ask stupid questions," I said through clenched teeth. "Now call this werewolf off, will ya?"

"Dare," Tyler said patiently, "just give her the bone."

"What bone?"

"The one in the grocery bag, stupid. Every time Laura buys groceries the butcher sends home a bone for Storm. As soon as she sees somebody with a grocery bag she comes running to get her bone. It's a big game to her."

"Some game," I muttered, gingerly reaching inside the bag and digging around until I came up with something about the size of a woolly mammoth's thigh bone. Obviously, the butcher had *seen* this dog. "Here, uh, Storm," I said kind of weakly, half expecting my right hand might go along as the appetizer. Storm's eyes lit up like thousand-watt bulbs and her mouth opened wide as she reached for the bone. As delicately as Gran would have picked up a cup of tea, she accepted her present and trotted off, her tail wagging like a victory flag.

Tyler looked up at me and gave me that innocent grin of his. "See, Dare," he said, "you've really got a way with dogs."

Laura kept us busy for the rest of the afternoon. Tyler used Laura's spare room all the time when he stayed here, but Laura sent us to the basement for an extra bed for me. By the time we got it set up and the rest of the furniture rearranged to make room for it, it was supper time.

I'd never really thought of Laura as the domestic type, so when she came up with a big platter of fried chicken I was kind of surprised. It was pretty good, too. But nobody ate very much. I was watching Ty. For a scrawny little kid he's usually got an awesome appetite. But not tonight. He was just sitting there staring at his plate. I figured this was the first time all day that things had slowed down enough for him to start thinking about Gran, probably the first time he'd let himself believe that she was really dead.

I forced myself to concentrate on eating. The food on my plate disappeared but it might as well have been cardboard for all I tasted it. I guess I was thinking too much, too. I wouldn't look at Laura but I could tell she wasn't eating much, either. She was watching us. Waiting. Waiting for us to fall apart so she could play mama? Well, keep waiting, Laura, I thought angrily. This kid doesn't fall apart.

Suddenly, Ty stood up. "I've got some homework," he said quietly. "May I be excused?"

Laura gave him a long look. Her face was softer than I'd ever seen it. "Sure, Tyler, if that's what you want," she said gently.

Tyler gathered up his dishes, scraped his uneaten food into the dog's dish and headed for our room. Laura and I sat, watching him go. Then Laura turned her attention on me. She had the kind of thoughtful expression that said she was going to start asking heavy questions. But I wasn't planning on answering them. I got up and followed Tyler. I didn't ask to be excused.

I didn't expect to find Ty doing his homework. He wasn't. He was standing staring out the window. I couldn't see his face but I thought he might be crying. I came up behind him. "Ty?" I said hesitantly. "You all right?"

He swallowed. "Yeah," he said in a low voice. He turned around then and I saw that he wasn't crying. Not quite. For a minute we just stood there looking at each other. I knew I should say something to him but I wasn't any good at this. Finally he broke the silence.

"Why, Dare? Why'd Gran have to die?"

I shook my head. "I dunno, Ty," I said. "Why does anybody have to die?" Why did Mom have to die? "Gran was pretty old," I added.

"No, she wasn't," he shot back, almost angrily. "She was only seventy-two. Lots of people live to be way older than that." He paused and then added thoughtfully, "I want to live to be real old and have grandchildren and great-grandchildren and all that stuff."

He was dead serious but I got a sudden mental picture of Ty with a long white beard holding a lap full of babies and telling them about the good old days and I couldn't help grinning. "Right on,

Gramps," I said, and in spite of himself Ty laughed. He was going to be all right, I thought. But then I started thinking about what he'd said. "Not me," I said. "I'd hate bein' old. I wanna live fast, love hard, die young and leave a beautiful memory."

I was kidding — mostly — but Ty didn't take it that way. "Don't, Dare," he said in a strange, hushed voice, and his face looked like I'd hit him.

"Don't what?" I asked, not understanding.

"Don't talk about dyin' and stuff."

"Hey, come on, Ty, lighten up. It's just an expression. I didn't mean anything by it."

His face didn't change. He just shook his head. "Sometimes I think you do mean it," he said softly.

Before I could take that in, there was a knock and the door opened. I hadn't thought I'd ever be so glad to see Laura. She gave us both a studying look and I could see she was reading the tension between us but not understanding the reason for it. Good luck, Laura, I thought. If you figure it out let me know.

I guess she gave up on it. "Come on, Ty," she said at last, "I've got to drive out to the west quarter with a block of salt. I need someone to open gates for me."

Tyler jumped up. "Sure, Laura," he said eagerly, and right then I knew that Laura didn't need a gate opener half as bad as Ty needed something to keep him busy for a while.

Nice move, Laura, I thought.

On her way to the door Laura looked back. "You coming, Dare?" she asked.

"No," I said. She didn't argue.

They were gone a long time. It was getting dark when I heard the truck pull into the yard. I figured they'd had time to do a lot of talking. I wondered what Laura had said to Ty. All the right things he needed to hear? All the things I didn't know how to say? I hoped so, because I still didn't have the answers — just a whole lot of questions. Suddenly I realized I didn't want to have to talk anymore at all tonight. I undressed and got into bed and pulled the covers up. By the time I heard the door open I was doing a real good job of playing possum.

Even with my eyes closed, I could feel Ty looking at me. I didn't move. At last he turned away. I heard him get into bed. A few minutes later I was sure he was asleep — and I was wide awake, listening to the coyotes howl in the distance.

At eleven I heard Laura putting the cats out and getting ready for bed. The house got quiet. Everything was peaceful — except for me. I was so wired I couldn't even stay in bed, let alone go to sleep.

A little before midnight it started to rain. I got up and stood by the window, staring out into the darkness. After a while it stopped raining. I glanced at my watch. One thirty-five glowed in the darkness. I looked out again. The moonlight was gleaming on the wet hood of Laura's truck.

I looked over at Ty, still sleeping like a baby. I

wondered again about what Laura had told him to-night. I remembered her arm around him at the hospital. And I knew that how I felt about Laura didn't matter. To Ty, she was the next best thing to the mother he'd barely even had — because of me. He needed Laura. Whether he knew it or not, he needed Laura a lot more than he needed me now.

I was talking myself into it.

Silently, I got dressed. My duffel bag was in the corner, still packed. I picked it up. I looked at Ty. I couldn't go without saying good-bye. But if I woke him up he'd never let me go. It was better this way. "Good luck, Tyler," I whispered, my throat aching.

I stepped into the dark hall. Laura had a good house for this. Nothing creaked or squeaked. I walked outside and over to the truck. A few drops of rain were still falling. Maybe that was why my face was wet.

I got in and pulled the door quietly shut. The keys still dangled from the ignition. You're a sucker, Laura, I thought with a bitter grin. But the grin faded out on me. I'd done a lot of things I wasn't real proud of, but I'd never stolen a car before.

I'm not stealing it, Laura, just borrowing it. That was the truth. As soon as I hit the city I'd park it and stick the keys in the mail for her. I wasn't rotten enough to really steal it. Besides, they'd track me down in no time, roaring around the country in a stolen truck.

I reached out to turn the key, then hesitated.

The lane ran right past the house. If I drove out there Laura was bound to wake up. But I could go out the back way, through the pasture. There was a gate down there where we'd found J.R. I could get out onto the road there.

I turned the key and the engine caught. Without turning on the lights, I eased out into the shadowy pasture. The moonlight wasn't as bright as I'd thought it would be. I was having trouble seeing.

Suddenly, there was a huge jolt. I slammed on the brakes. Now you've done it, Dare. You must have run over a cow, at least. I got out cautiously. No cow corpses. I breathed a sigh of relief. Then I saw the victim. A brand-new block of blue cow salt, half buried in the soft ground. I dug it out and moved it out of the way.

I was just getting back in when, somewhere behind me, a yard light switched on. Great! I slammed the door and gunned it. The big engine roared and we bounced wildly over the uneven ground. I could see the gate. Only another hundred yards. But all of a sudden, the truck started slowing down. I floored it and the engine roared louder — but the truck moved still slower. Something was dragging it down. I opened the window to see what was going on — and caught a big gob of mud right in the eye. And then I finally caught on. The wheels were going around but I wasn't going anywhere. I was stuck. Stuck right up to the hubcaps and sinking fast. I rammed it into reverse and stepped on the gas. The tires howled and mud flew. But we didn't move. Swearing, I pounded my fist on the dash and threw it into drive again. Drive, reverse, drive, reverse.

A light hit me in the face, almost blinding me. Game over. I cut the engine. The light angled down out of my eyes and I could see again. It was Laura, of course, wearing a beat-up cowboy hat, a long yellow rain slicker and her pajamas, tucked into the top of a pair of men's rubber boots. She was standing there holding a flashlight and shaking her head as she studied the buried truck.

"Now that was pretty stupid, Dare," she said calmly. "This thing's a four by four; it's not a tank. There are things it won't go through. This bog right here happens to be one of them."

"So go ahead and call the cops," I said sullenly, staring at the steering wheel.

"The cops?" Laura barked. "What do I want with the cops in the middle of the night?"

I looked up at her. "I just stole your truck." I said tiredly. "People usually think that's reason enough to call the cops."

Laura gave a snort of laughter. "You mean you tried to steal my truck. You're going to have to smarten up a lot before you get good at this. Anyway, the cops have got nothing to do with this. It wasn't their truck you tried to steal. It was mine. And you'll deal with me. Now get out of there and get back up to the house before I catch my death of cold." She glanced up the slope toward the house and added, "And now you've got Tyler out here slopping around in the wet, too."

I looked. Ty was just stumbling sleepily down the hill toward us, his jean jacket over his pajamas. He looked the situation over but for once he didn't ask a single question. From the look he gave me I figured he understood all too well what had happened.

We all trudged silently back to the house. Laura hung up her hat and raincoat and was just turning toward her bedroom when she paused and gave me a hard look.

"The keys are in the ton truck, too," she said grumpily. "You planning on trying again tonight?"

I could feel my face starting to burn. I met her look reluctantly. "No," I said, my voice coming out more defiant than sorry.

"Good. Then maybe we can all get some sleep." She marched into her bedroom and slammed the door.

There was nothing left to do but go to bed. Tyler and I walked silently down to our room. Without looking in his direction, I undressed, fell into bed and killed the light, hoping he'd get the message that I was in no mood to talk.

Two minutes later his voice cut the silence. "Dare?"

"What?" I muttered.

"You gonna try to run out on me again?" Even in the darkness I could feel those serious gray eyes burning a hole in me. When it came to laying on a guilt trip . . .

"Look," I said, "if I leave, when I leave, I'm not takin' you, Ty. That's final."

"But — "

I cut him off. "Where I'm goin' it's gonna be rough and I don't want you taggin' along behind me all the time." I was playing rough, meaning the words to hurt and hating myself for saying them. But it was the only way to get through to him.

He was quiet for a long time and I figured that he'd finally given up. But then he started talking again. "If you go without me, I'll follow you," he said, and something in his voice made me believe it. He wasn't bluffing. And that screwed up my plans real good.

I'd had it all figured out. Wherever I went I could get along somehow. I was big enough to pass for seventeen or eighteen. I could get a job. And even if I couldn't, I'd find a way to survive. Even seven years in Crossing hadn't completely knocked the streetwise out of me . . .

But Ty? Twelve years old, too good-looking for his own good and so innocent he'd trust the devil himself. Just thinking about Ty alone on the big-city streets made me go cold. He didn't belong there. He belonged here. And that meant I was trapped. Life was such a rip-off. The whole world was full of people who wanted somebody to need them. Me, I just wanted to be a loner and what did

I get? A kid brother who thought I was the Lone Ranger and who just wanted to hang around me and be Tonto.

But I was too tired to fight it anymore. "Okay, Ty," I said at last. "You win. I'll stick around as long as you need me." I reached across the narrow space between our beds and gave his bony shoulder a squeeze.

"I knew you would," he said softly. Five minutes later he was asleep.

Chapter 9

The next day was Saturday. We spent the early morning getting the truck out. When I saw that mudhole in daylight, I couldn't believe it. It looked like something the dinosaurs would have wallowed in. It took a real special kind of fool to drive into a place like that. Laura got on the tractor.

She hooked a long cable onto the front bumper of the truck and then onto the drawbar of the tractor.

"Want me to drive the truck?" I asked, real quiet.

Laura tossed her head. "Not likely," she said. "You already tried driving and look where it got you. Tyler can drive. You can push."

"I can what?" I squawked, staring at that evil muck.

"You heard me, Sunshine. Pushing is done by getting close to the vehicle. Now move it!" she yelled, revving up the tractor.

The slop was above my knees. I felt it trickling coldly inside my sneakers and every step I took made a sucking noise like a toilet plunger. Too mad to even swear, I threw my shoulder against the tailgate and started to push. Laura started to pull. Ty hit the gas, spun the tires and sent a sheet of liquid mud flying in the air. Most of it landed on me. Before I could even react to that, the tires hit solid footing and that truck shot forward like a racehorse. Before I could jerk my feet loose from the mud the momentum of my push threw me forward. I landed face first in the muck.

Laura stopped the tractor and walked back as I dragged myself, dripping, to my feet. She shook her head. "Dirty business this truck stealing, isn't it, Dare?" she said, straight-faced. "Go on up to the house and wash up," she added. "Come on, Ty, let's see how Dolly Parton's calf is doing since we're here."

I trudged up the hill to the house, pulled my ruined sneakers off on the back step and headed for the bathroom to clean up. A few minutes later I came out in clean clothes — and a whole lot better mood. I was almost ready to forgive Laura when she met me at the kitchen door with a mop.

"Here," she said, shoving it into my hand, "you've got work to do."

My eyes followed hers down the long muddy trail my oozing socks had made to the bathroom.

I stared at her. "I don't know how to do housework," I said. Gran had never made us clean the house. That was women's work, I thought. But some instinct for survival told me not to say *that* to Laura.

"Takes a strong back and a weak mind," she growled, handing me a bucket to go with the mop. "You should be good at it. And anybody who can handle that big motorcycle I see you riding shouldn't have too much trouble figuring out a washing machine. You can work on your clothes after you finish the floor. Come on, Tyler, let's get out of his way."

Without another word, Laura marched outside. Tyler followed, trying not too successfully to keep from grinning as he looked back over his shoulder at his big, dangerous brother — holding a deadly mop.

Cleaning that floor took the rest of the morning. Next time, Laura, I thought, just go ahead and call the cops. If you don't, I will. Going to jail couldn't be this bad.

By the time I got finished, I was in such a rotten mood I almost passed up lunch. But all that housework had worked me up a good appetite. So I ate — but I didn't talk. I figured I was going to disappear for the rest of the day as soon as I was done eating.

Unfortunately, Laura had other ideas. She finished wiping the table off, threw the dishcloth in the sink and fastened a stern look on me. "Well, Dare," she said, "if you're going to be any earthly use around this place you're going to need a horse."

Wrong on two counts, Laura, I thought, returning the look. I don't plan on being any use around here and I sure don't need a horse.

Five minutes later, I was standing in the barn, watching as Laura led out a big, sleepy-looking bay gelding. "This is Chief," she said. "He's been around long enough to know the ropes. He'll teach you all you need to know about horses."

Ty had wandered out and now he put in his two bits' worth. "Yeah, Dare, I learned to ride on him. He's pretty safe for beginners."

I gave him a dirty glare. Just what I needed. A horse that my baby brother had outgrown.

"Here," Laura said, holding out the halter rope. "Take him."

I shook my head. "I don't like horses," I said. Right then Chief decided to shake his head, too — and blow his nose. He gave a loud snort and a cool shower of horse snot landed all over me.

Laura laughed. "See, Dare, he doesn't like you, either. It should work out fine." She glanced at her watch. "You go ahead and get to know him. Ty'll show you the ropes. I've got work to do." She started walking away. "Oh," she added over her shoulder, "your saddle is the first one on the rack."

My saddle? I was just passing through. What did I need with a saddle?

Before I'd even finished that thought there was a sudden sound of splintering wood from behind the barn, followed by a loud, defiant whinny. Then a couple more crashes and the hoofbeats of a galloping horse.

Laura froze in her tracks, muttered a few words I didn't think teachers were supposed to know and went tearing out the back door. Ty was right on her heels and I abandoned Chief and took off after them both.

I ran out the door just in time to catch a glimpse of a streak of silver blue disappearing into the woods at the edge of the pasture. In front of us it looked like a tornado had just gone through. Three rails were knocked off the corral fence and the top one was smashed to pieces.

"What happened?" I asked.

Laura stood there, her hands on her hips, shaking her head. "Smoke happened," she said, in a tone that held as much admiration as disgust. "That's the second time he's broke jail this spring." She nudged a broken rail with the toe of her boot. "That horse can sure take apart a corral when he sets his mind to it."

I didn't know much about Laura's horses but I had heard of Smoke — about a thousand times — from Tyler. His registered name was Doc's Smokin' Joe and he was a three-year-old quarter horse stallion. A blue roan, which is supposed to be kind of rare, I guess. Anyhow, according to Ty, Smoke was the greatest horse that ever lived and Laura was planning on using him to start a whole line of blue roans — if she could keep track of him long enough. Tyler had said Smoke had a wild streak.

"We gonna go after him?" Tyler asked eagerly.

Laura shook her head. "No, not right now. I've got work that can't wait. He'll be all right out with the mares and colts. They'll all come up one of these days. We'll get him then. Besides, we've got to fix the fence before we put him back in here." She walked off toward the tractor shed.

"If that horse is so much trouble, why does she like him so much?" I asked Tyler as the two of us headed back into the barn.

He gave me a thoughtful look. Then, "That's probably why," he said. I was still trying to sort that answer out when he said, "I'm gonna ride out and check on the cattle. Wanna come? Maybe we'll even see Smoke on the way."

I hesitated. I didn't think I wanted to ride anywhere on Chief but it might beat sitting around here. If I didn't look busy, Laura would probably find some work for me.

I shrugged. "Yeah, I guess — *if* you show me how to get the saddle on this overgrown camel."

"You got it, Dare," he said, laughing.

Ty talked a blue streak while we rode. From the mood he was in, I think he figured I must be starting to accept living with Laura. He had another thing coming, but I let it go for now. It was a nice day. I was almost enjoying the ride — except that Chief was the roughest ride next to accidentally getting trapped in a blender. When he trotted the needle went right off the end of the Richter scale.

Ty jumped off, dropped Chance's reins and

opened a gate. She just stood and waited for him. We rode on. "Chief really is a great old horse," he was saying. "He's only got one bad habit to watch out for."

Aside from blowing his nose in your face? I wondered, but Ty went on explaining. "He won't ground tie," he said. I was supposed to ask what that meant. But I was sick of having my kid brother explain things to me.

I just shrugged. "I knew that."

Ty wanted to ride another couple of miles, but since we were in the cattle pasture now we wouldn't see Smoke and I'd had enough of riding this portable milkshake machine. I headed back to the barn.

Halfway there, I had to open that gate again. I got off, led Chief through and dropped the reins while I closed it. As I walked up to him to get back on, he suddenly looked up, threw his head high in the air so the reins were barely touching the ground and took off at a gallop for home. I just stood there, staring after him — and thinking up a few new names for him, too.

I started walking home. I was nearly there when Tyler caught up to me. "What'd you do with your horse?" he asked, sounding like he suspected I'd eaten him for supper.

I told him, in detail, what that four-legged streak of misery had done to me.

Ty looked at me like I was one brick short of a load. "Told you he wouldn't ground tie," he said.

"I didn't ground tie him," I shot back angrily. "I just dropped the reins like you did at the gate."

"Dare," Tyler said, "that *is* ground tying."

Just then Laura came out of the tractor shed and saw me come walking in. I could see the wheels going around in her head and I knew she had figured out what had happened. But all she said was, "Now what, Dare? You get the horse stuck, too?"

Chapter 10

The rest of the weekend went by fast. With final exams starting Monday, Tyler and I ended up studying most of Sunday. Tyler did it because he was Tyler and maybe because it kept him from thinking about Gran so much. I did it because I didn't have much choice. I made a halfhearted suggestion to Laura that I'd maybe just hitchhike into town and see how Keith was doing but I almost got blown out of the water for my trouble. I did not need to go to town, I did not need to see Keith. And furthermore, as Laura put it, she had risked life and limb, not to mention future subbing jobs, to convince the principal that, under the circumstances, my behavior Friday was not a good enough reason to expel me forever. Therefore, the least I could do was to hit the books and see if I might accidentally pass an exam or two.

It was after supper and I was lying on my bed staring empty-eyed at my science text when Tyler came in and sat down on his bed. He didn't say anything and I wasn't feeling talkative, either, so

I just kept on pretending to read. Finally he broke the silence.

"You got any money, Dare?" That was about the last question I expected to hear from him. He knows how long money usually lasts me.

I sat up and emptied my pockets. "Sure, Ty, I'm loaded. Seventy-five cents and one and a half matches."

I lay back and started reading again but then I got curious. "How much do you need?" I asked.

"Twenty-five dollars."

I sat up. "Twenty-five bucks? Hey, your lifestyle's gettin' more expensive. What happened? You discover women or something?"

I gave him a teasing grin and waited for him to explode. Ty doesn't believe in girls — yet.

But he never turned a hair. He just shook his head and then said quietly, "It's for Gran. We gotta get her some flowers."

My grin faded. I'd been avoiding even thinking about the funeral. I didn't want to go. If it hadn't been for Ty I knew I wouldn't go. I wasn't sure I could handle another funeral. But I couldn't let him go without me. And he was right, Gran should have flowers. I'd had flowers for Mom. The nurse had bought them for me. The nurse who'd volunteered to go with me to the funeral. Neither the doctor who was looking after me nor the Social Services people wanted to let me go. They didn't figure a funeral was any place for a seven-year-old who was still half in shock from the fire.

It was the hospital psychologist who talked them into it. She said if I wanted to go so bad they'd better let me go. I heard her talking to them about how I needed it for "resolution of grief" or something like that. I didn't even know what that meant. All I knew was that they were going to put my mom in the ground and if it wasn't for me she wouldn't be dead. I had to be there to say good-bye — and tell her I was sorry.

Ty's voice jerked me back to the present. "I went to the flower shop," he was saying, "but the nice ones for funerals cost forty dollars."

I looked at Ty with new respect. He may be my kid brother, but he's the one who does the grown-up stuff.

"I've only got fifteen so far," he went on.

"Where'd you get that much?" I asked.

Ty's gaze dropped to the floor guiltily. If it had been anyone but him, I would have thought he must have stolen the money. "I, uh, sold my Stetson to Chuck Munez at school Friday," he said softly. "He's had his eye on it ever since I got it." I stared at him unbelievingly. That was like hearing he'd sold his right hand. He'd decided to take a shot at steer riding at the rodeo last year and I guess the hat's a real important part of playing cowboy. Gran couldn't afford to buy him one — she thought the whole idea was dumb anyway — so Laura bought it for him. For helping her show her horses at the fair, she said. He'd been treating it like pure gold ever since. I should know. I accidentally sat on it once and almost got my lights punched out.

He looked up at me half defiantly, like he expected me to be mad at him or something. "Anyway," he said, "it's not enough. I'm gonna have to ask Laura for a loan."

"No!" I said angrily, standing up and facing him. "You're not gonna ask Laura. This doesn't have nothin' to do with Laura. It's our problem, not hers."

Ty gave me a level look. "Okay then, Dare. You got any better ideas?"

For a minute I didn't answer. I just paced, trying to think. There had to be an answer. And suddenly it hit me. I *did* have some money. Enough money. Twenty-five dollars. The money I owed to Keith for the concert ticket. I'd put it away a long time ago where I wouldn't see it and get any ideas about spending it. I went over to the closet and got out my leather jacket — the one I usually just wear for riding Keith's bike. I opened the front snap pocket and breathed a sigh of relief. The money was there, right where I'd put it. I turned back to Ty.

"Here," I said, tossing the bills onto the bed beside him. He smoothed them out carefully and counted them and then his face lit up.

"It's enough," he said softly, but then a worried frown crossed his face. "Where'd you get it?" he asked suspiciously.

"Don't worry," I said, "I got it legal. I've been savin' it for a rainy day."

Ty got the flowers. Red roses. They looked real

nice there on the casket. I should know. I sat there in the front seat of the church and never took my eyes off those flowers. That's how I got through the funeral. Froze up solid inside and went through the motions like a robot.

Oh, I noticed things, all right. Things like how almost everyone in the church was old — which figured, since most of Gran's friends were around her age. Tyler and I were the only kids there. Everybody stared at us like we were Exhibit A. I stared back at them as we walked in. But I didn't really see them. 'Cause I wasn't really there.

The whole thing was rough on Ty. Especially at the cemetery when they put Gran in the ground. He cried his guts out all through that part. I could understand. That was when I'd cried hardest, too, at Mom's funeral.

But I didn't cry at Gran's funeral. I was all done with that kind of crying. I saw the old ladies look at me and whisper and I figured they were talking about how hard and unfeeling that oldest Jamieson boy was. You got it, ladies, I thought.

Ty seemed a lot better after the funeral. Like he'd been through the worst and got the crying over with. There were still a couple of exams to write and that gave him something to think about. Between studying and helping Laura he didn't have much time for missing Gran. It seemed pretty weird, but *I* was the one who was going nuts.

Exams finished at noon on Friday and by Friday night I'd had about all of this good, clean country living I could stand. If I had to listen to Ty and Laura discuss halter breaking and hoof trimming and how the alfalfa was growing for one more evening I was going to be climbing the walls.

But being bored out of my mind wasn't the worst part. Even if I could stand the evenings, the nights would kill me. I couldn't sleep. No matter how late I stayed awake reading or watching TV — believe it or not, Laura didn't send me off to bed at nine o'clock — I'd still go to bed so tensed up I was about ready to explode. Then I'd lie awake for hours trying to sort out my life. Wondering what was going to happen next. Being at Laura's was bad enough, but I knew it was only temporary. After that, things could get worse.

What was really getting to me, though, was that I'd started dreaming again — about Mom. I'd been over that for years now but ever since Gran's funeral it had been happening again. I guess I just got to thinking too much. Now, even if I could go to sleep, I was scared to let myself do it. I needed to go somewhere, do something, or I was going to blow up.

That's what was on my mind when the phone rang. I argued with myself about even answering it. It was probably one of Laura's farmer friends wanting to discuss the price of horse manure or something. But curiosity got the better of me. On the fourth ring I picked it up. It was Keith.

"Hey, man, you took your sweet time answering. I was sure Old Lady McConnell was going to pick it up and I was getting ready to hang up real fast if she did." He paused. Then, "She there listening to you?"

"Naw, she and Ty are out watching the grass grow or something."

"Sounds about her speed," Keith said sarcastically. "So how's life in the country, Dare?" I could tell by his tone of voice that he already knew how much I was enjoying this.

"The pits," I said, groaning. "The absolute, end-of-the-world pits."

"No kiddin'. Well, how'd you *really* like to go to the Pits?"

"What?"

"You know, the Pits. There's a big end-of-school party out there tonight."

Crossing isn't exactly the entertainment capital of the world. Parties at the Pits were big-time stuff. On a Friday night half the kids that went to Crossing High School showed up — the wild half. The ones whose parents didn't care where they were and the ones who were good enough liars to convince their parents they were going someplace else. The strict parents wouldn't let their kids get within a mile of the place. In Laura's case, I had a feeling the distance would be more like two miles.

Keith must have been reading my mind. "So," he said, his voice challenging, "will Laura let you come?"

"Not very likely."

He started to say something but I cut him off.

"So pick me up at Laura's corner at ten."

Keith laughed. "Right on, man."

I hung up the phone and turned around — and there was Ty, leaning against the door frame and not missing a thing.

He shook his head solemnly. "Laura won't like it."

"Laura won't even know unless you rat on me."

He gave me an insulted look. "I never used to rat to Gran, did I?"

I had to admit it, he never had. "Okay," I said, "here's the deal."

At a quarter to ten we were in our room. We'd been really tired tonight and gone to bed early.

I stood on top of Ty's bed and opened the window wide and then carefully lifted out the screen. "See ya, kid," I whispered as I climbed out.

"Don't do anything I wouldn't do," Ty warned.

I laughed as I dropped silently to the ground. If I followed that advice I might as well spend the evening in a monastery.

Chapter 11

The party was just getting going when Keith and I rode in on the Shadow. There were a lot of cars parked in a big circle with all the radios tuned to AM 106 and really cranked so the rock sound echoed off the walls of the old gravel pit and practically shook the ground. Some kids were building a big fire so we could roast some wieners — and probably somebody's sneakers — later on.

It was shaping up like a regular Pits party, a little drinking, a little bragging and lie swapping, a few couples necking, a couple of fistfights — and after a few bottles of beer, the old argument. Could anybody actually drive up that steep west wall of the biggest pit? Every party somebody got drunk enough to try it in a four by four. They usually powered out halfway up and slid back down, but once in a while somebody turned up with something with enough power to make it close to the top. But nobody had ever made it *over* the top. The angle gets too steep and they roll. A couple of trucks have been totaled that way. A few years ago a kid got killed.

That's not for me. I'm not about to risk rolling down there in a sardine can of mashed metal.

Keith had disappeared a long time ago to try to get his old girlfriend over not speaking to him, and I'd been hanging out with a bunch of older guys who had a good beer supply. They'd been kicking around the subject of climbing that bank for half the night.

Finally Big Dave Callahan stood up, weaved back and forth a little and declared in a loud voice, "Ain't no truck in Crossing can do it and none of you little wimps that's man enough to try, anyhow."

I was feeling just good enough to take that personally. "Yeah?" I said, standing up, too. "Maybe there ain't a truck but I've got a bike that'll do it."

They all turned to look at me. I was younger than the rest of them by a couple of years and usually I knew enough to keep my mouth shut.

"Jamieson," Big Dave said with a sneer, "you couldn't ride that Honda over a curb without fallin' off."

"Oh, yeah?" I had my fist doubled up to punch him when Joe Lefleur, a big, quiet Indian kid, grabbed my arm.

"Don't get mad," he said, low voiced. "Get even. Get the bike and do it."

I took a quick glance around. Keith was nowhere in sight. I figured he'd be here fast enough when he heard the bike start up but by then it would be too late. I got on the bike, took a deep breath and turned the key. The roar of that engine almost drowned out the pounding beat of the car stereos as I revved it up and started making a big circle away from the wall of the pit. In the firelight I caught glimpses of kids starting to gather and point and stare in my direction. Once I caught the unmistakable scrawny silhouette of Keith. He was waving his arms and running in my direction. I looked the other way.

Keith didn't exist anymore. The yelling crowd of rowdy kids was gone. Now it was just me and the bike — and the steep, rocky side of the pit. And I wasn't me any more. I was part of the bike. Metal. Indestructible. Like Robocop. A machine with a human soul. I was gaining speed. The tires hit the loose gravel at the bottom of the slope, spraying it out behind like dust. Then they dug in, and that bike just kept burning up that hill. Halfway and it still wasn't slowing down. Three-quarters. The momentum was easing off a little but I was still moving fast. The last pitch. Almost straight up. The speed was bleeding off now. Come on, Dare. Think it through. Use what you learned when you tried Kagan's Butte.

Kagan's Butte! It was the first time tonight that incident had even crossed my mind. What had I learned at Kagan's Butte? Only one thing. It hurts like hell when you fall.

Desperately, I leaned into that bank. I was almost carrying the bike as the top wheel crawled over the lip of the bank. The back wheel spun wildy, half in thin air, caught a half-buried rock, dug in and threw the bike up onto the flat grassland above. I landed off balance and the bike and I wound up in a heap on the ground. On the ground *above* the Pits.

"Yahoo!" I screamed from the rim of the pit. Fifty kids down below cheered as I waved to them. I couldn't help wondering if Keith was one of them.

Poor old Keith wouldn't know whether to hug me or slug me. His bike had just become King of the Hill. His buddy, me, had just become a hero — for the next hour at least. I climbed back on the bike and roared back to the party — taking the long, winding trail back down. I did quite a bit of celebrating in the next little while. So much I kind of lost track of time.

It wasn't until Keith and a couple of other guys finally sat me on the bike that I hazily checked my watch. It said three-thirty.

Keith dropped me at the corner again and the half-mile walk did a lot to clear my brain. By the time I reached the house I was remembering my plan of action. Quietly, I edged around the corner of the house and started working my way along to our bedroom.

All of a sudden, I got a being-watched feeling. I looked over my shoulder. Oh, no. It was instant-replay time. Storm was stalking me again. She was standing there with her head cocked sideways giving me one of those humans-sure-are-weird looks that only a dog can give. I could see she was trying to decide whether to treat this as a breaking-and-entering-case or just write it off to my general feeblemindedness. She gave one low, experimental bark.

"Sh!" I whispered. "Trust me, Storm, I know what I'm doin'. Go chase the coyotes."

That was a mistake. "Coyotes" was second only in importance to "eat" in Storm's vocabulary. Her ears shot straight up, she growled deep in her throat and she stuck her nose in the air testing for a whiff of passing coyote. Then she started to bark — big, deep, loud German shepherd barks.

Smooth move, Dare, I told myself, crouching unsteadily between a big, bad-tempered rosebush and the side of the house and expecting Laura to come roaring around the corner any minute with the shotgun.

I reached up to get my hand over the window ledge and start pulling myself in — and touched screen. How did the screen get back in the window? There was no way I could lift it out from here. "Ty!" I hissed in a loud whisper. Nothing. "Tyler!"

Soft footsteps inside. "Dare? Is that you?"

I thought of fratricide again. "No, it's Jack the Ripper and you're going to be my next victim if I ever lay my hands on you. Let me in."

He didn't answer but I heard him slowly begin

to work the screen loose. Finally I felt it move away from my hand. I dragged myself up, over the sill and in. "What'd you go and put the screen back in for?" I growled. "You almost got me caught."

Ty gave me an innocent look. "The mosquitoes were getting in," he explained calmly. I just shook my head. Sometimes Ty reminded me of Mr. Spock on the old *Star Trek*. A Vulcan. Born to be logical. If the mosquitoes are getting in, put in the screen. Never mind the details.

"And how did you figure I was going to get in?"

Ty climbed back into bed. "Ever hear of doors, Dare?" he asked, poker-faced as usual. All of a sudden, we both burst out laughing.

"You looked pretty funny out there behind the rosebush," he said.

I grabbed my pillow and heaved it at him. He ducked and knocked the lamp over.

"Hey!" Laura's voice rasped angrily from down the hall. "You two settle down in there. It's four o'clock in the morning and between you and the dog I'd like to know how anybody's supposed to sleep around here. Get that light out. Morning'll be here soon enough." Her door slammed and everything was quiet for a minute.

Then Ty shot me one of his serious looks. "Get to bed, Dare," he said sternly, echoing Laura's tone. "It's four o'clock in the morning. You're being a bad influence on me." He winked, set the lamp upright and turned it off.

I fell into bed, just beginning to realize how tired I was — and starting to feel a little like I might be coming down with something. But I'd done it. For once I'd outfoxed Laura. I fell asleep fast for a change — with a grin on my face.

Chapter 12

It felt like I'd been asleep about five minutes when the earthquake started. At first I was so spaced I thought it must be an earthquake. What else would be shaking me like this in the middle of the night? I moaned and tried to bury my head under the pillow. If I was going to die, let me die comfortable. But then something grabbed the pillow and tore it out of my hands. Even for an earthquake this was getting a little far out. I risked opening one eye. That was a mistake. A ray of sunlight coming through the window zapped me and I closed the eye fast. But why was the sun shining in the middle of the night? Groggily, I half sat up. "What time is it, anyhow?" I muttered, mainly to myself.

"Quarter to seven," Laura's voice answered briskly, sounding like she'd been awake for hours. "You want any breakfast you've got exactly five minutes to be up, dressed and at the table."

Breakfast? The word had an obscene sound right then. "Don't want any," I groaned, trying to bury myself in the safe darkness of the blankets.

"Okay, suit yourself, Dare, but we've got a long day of fencing ahead of us. You're going to be pretty hungry before you get another chance to eat."

I sat up again slowly. This time I opened both eyes — and stared at Laura. "Fencing?" I repeated stupidly, shaking off a mental picture of a couple of guys dancing around in ballet pants having sword fights. The other kind of fencing was no improvement, though. "I don't know nothin' about fencing," I said.

Laura smiled. "You will by tonight," she said in a dangerously pleasant voice.

"Oh, no, I ain't buildin' any fence." My temper was starting to warm up a little. I was just awake enough to discover that my head felt like a Halloween pumpkin — complete with jagged holes and a fire inside.

"Oh," Laura said calmly. "And what do you have in mind for this morning then?"

"Sleep," I mumbled, burying my head in my hands. "I think I'm comin' down with something."

Laura didn't say anything for a moment and when I looked up at her she reached out and laid her cool hand on my forehead. It felt good. Maybe old Laura really did have a soft side to her. Maybe if I . . .

"All you're coming down with is what you deserve after last night." Laura's voice had gone rock hard. "You figure you're man enough to stay out partying half the night, you better be man enough to do a day's work the next day." Suddenly she bent down, gathered up the trail of clothes I'd shed before I fell into bed last night, bundled them into a solid lump and threw them at me. "You get yourself into these and be ready to roll in five minutes or I'll be back." She stalked toward the door, then stopped and threw one last, scornful glance over her shoulder. "And from now on, if you can't stand the heat, stay out of the kitchen." The door slammed behind her.

I just shook my aching head, regretfully remembering how I'd "fooled" Laura last night.

I was still only about half conscious and half dressed when I stumbled into the kitchen, but I did manage to make my eyes focus on the clock above the sink. I'd made it in four and a half minutes. Why I'd made it at all was more than I knew. Except that right now I just wasn't up to calling Laura's bluff.

I collapsed in the chair next to Ty, who was just polishing off a big, gooey stack of pancakes. He glanced over at me.

"S'good, Dare," he mumbled through a mouthful. "Wan' some?" He held up a forkful that dripped syrup and the remains of a fried egg.

My stomach lurched and I clapped my hand over my mouth and swallowed hard. Ty just sat there, studying me with scientific interest and waiting for an answer. Finally he got the message. "Guess not, huh?" His face was dead serious but I had a feeling he was laughing inside. Some day, kid, I thought weakly, but before I could finish thinking Laura slammed a mug of black coffee down in front of me.

"Drink this, then grab your jacket and the work gloves I left by the door for you. Come on, Ty. If you're finished you can help me load the tools in the truck."

"Okay, Laura." Ty stuck his dishes in the dishwasher and trotted after her like an obedient puppy. I watched them go. Then I laid my head beside my coffee mug. The table was cool and comfortable.

The blast of the truck horn shot through my head like a steel-pointed arrow. I groaned and sat up halfway straight. Go away. Leave me alone. Another blast. Two blasts. One long, one short. No. No more. I'm comin', I'm comin'. I gulped some coffee too fast, burned my tongue and gave up. I headed for the door, grabbing my jacket from the hook as I went by.

The back of the truck was full of fence posts, rolls of barbed wire and a bunch of tools that looked like they'd been borrowed from a torture chamber. Laura and Ty were in the front, waiting. In between spells of leaning on the horn, Laura was impatiently drumming her fingers on the steering wheel. I jerked open the door and fell into the seat next to Ty. Laura gave me a quick glance. "You got everything?" she asked shortly.

Everything? What was everything? I was here. That was enough. "Yeah," I said, not looking at Laura. She nodded, slammed the truck into gear and took off down the rough back trail like it was a four-lane highway. My head . . .

We drove a couple of miles, I guess, all the way

to the west end of Laura's land and on into the grazing land she leases for summer pasture. Finally, at a corner where two barbed-wire fences met, she stopped the truck. "Okay, Dare, hit the ground," she ordered, already half out of the truck herself. I looked around. The land was low and swampy here. Every so often, through the tall grass, I could see the gleam of water, and even through the truck's dirty window I could see the swarms of mosquitoes out there.

I looked at Laura. "What am I supposed to do?" I asked rebelliously.

Laura threw me an impatient glance. "You're going to take down that half mile of fence we just passed so we can replace all these old rotten posts and then string new wire. Hurry up. I want to show you what to do and I haven't got all day."

"Me neither," I muttered under my breath and climbed out of the truck — slow. Slow enough to rattle Laura's chain a little. She knew I was doing it on purpose, and I wanted her to know. It was a way of fighting back that didn't take a whole lot of energy.

By the time I'd sauntered around to the back she had gathered up the hammer and fencing pliers and was already attacking the fence. Metal screeched as she jerked the staple out of the post and the wire sagged loose. She threw the staple in an old paint can and moved on to the next post. I followed behind reluctantly.

"Okay," she said, "this is what you do first. Get

all the staples out. Just one wire at a time, though, or you'll have a tangle of wire you'll never sort out." She moved on to the next post and the next, ripping out staples while I just stood there, feeding the mosquitoes and trying to keep my eyes open. Laura came back to the corner post. She took the pliers and untied the end of the wire from the post. A long stretch of loose wire sagged to the ground.

"Now," she said, putting down the pliers and staple can, "this is how you roll up the wire." She glanced over her shoulder and saw me standing there staring into space and scratching mosquito bites. "Darren!" she bellowed. "Wake up and get over here." I ambled over, grinning to myself. Laura's cool was wearing a little thin.

I slouched beside her, watching halfheartedly as she picked up the end of the wire and bent it into a loop about the size of a coiled lariat rope. Then she wrapped the end of the wire around the loop to keep it from uncoiling. "Now comes the tricky part. Wire won't stay coiled like rope. It's stiff and if you're not careful, all of a sudden your whole roll will uncoil like a spring and you'll be right back where you started. So you've got to sort of weave each new loop from side to side to make sure it catches on the barbs of the loop before . . ." She shot a sharp look at me. "You watching this?"

"Yeah." My eyes fixed glassily on her hands in their heavy work gloves and I thought how glad I was going to be to get out of this place.

"Well, you better be," Laura said, "because in

about five minutes you're going to be on your own here while Tyler and I go up another mile and start dropping these posts off." She turned her attention back to the wire. "See how it works? Catch it over here and then work it over." A mosquito about the size of an army helicopter landed on my arm, dug in and started siphoning blood like a vampire. I swatted him. Laura sighed and looked up again.

"Where's your jacket?" she asked impatiently.

I shrugged. "Truck, I guess."

"Well, go get it. You can't swat mosquitoes and concentrate on what you're doing at the same time." I wandered over and picked up the jacket. Ty was standing by the truck, waiting for Laura. "You keep movin' at that speed we might get done by Christmas," he said sarcastically.

I gave him a cold stare. "When I need your comments, I'll let you know." He returned the stare. I pulled the jacket on slowly and headed back to the fence. My kid brother is changing, I thought.

Laura glanced at the jacket. "That's better. Now you take over and see how you do." She handed me the roll of wire. Gingerly, I closed my hand around the barb-studded coil, but Laura stopped me.

"No," she snapped, her voice sharp with anger. "You don't handle barbed wire bare-handed or it'll tear you to pieces. Where are the gloves I gave you?" Good question. The last I'd seen of them they'd been lying on the floor by the back door. I didn't remember picking them up.

"Forgot 'em," I said.

Laura threw the coil of wire on the ground. "You forgot! Well, that's just great. So far this morning you've had exactly one responsiblity. To get yourself up, properly dressed and out here. And you've scored a big zero on even that. Well, I've got too much to do to spend any more time baby-sitting you, and I need the truck to haul these posts up the line. The first thing you can do is start walking home after those gloves. At the rate you move, Tyler and I will probably be almost done with that other stretch of fence by the time you get back." She paused, and the look she gave me was pure contempt. "But you could try to at least get started before we have to come and finish the job for you."

Without another look in my direction she stalked over to the truck and opened the door. "Let's go, Ty," she ordered. He hesitated a minute, looking back at me. Then he got in. Both doors slammed and the way Laura spun out of there she would have laid rubber all over the highway.

Chapter 13

I stood and watched the truck churn its way down the muddy fence line and finally top a little hill and disappear on the other side. Then it was just me — and the mosquitoes. I looked down the long trail that led back to the house. Two miles of mud and mosquitoes under a hot June sun? All that before I even got back to start on the stupid wire? But who said I was coming back? I'd walk, all right. And just keep walking. I wasn't born to be Laura's slave. I started out.

I got maybe a hundred yards before I stopped. I'm not sure what stopped me. Maybe the fact that I hate walking as much as anything. But there was something else that wouldn't stop nagging at me. The look Laura had given me just before she drove away. It had taken quite a while but all of a sudden I understood what that look had meant. She'd written me off. Laura McConnell had finally decided I wasn't worth the trouble anymore. She didn't just think I *wouldn't* do the job she'd thrown at me. She thought I *couldn't* do it. My kid brother probably could. But he was different. He wasn't gutless and useless and . . .

Suddenly, I turned around. Okay, Laura, just watch. I won't do it your way, but I'll do it. I wasn't about to spend half the day walking back and forth for a pair of stupid gloves. I jogged back to where Laura had left off, grabbed the pliers and the can and started down the fence line, ripping staples out. All the staples. None of this one-wire-at-a-time stuff. That was too slow. Get all the wire loose first. I'd sort it out later.

It fell into a rhythm. Grab the staple with the pliers, jerk it loose, dump it in the can. Three times for every post. It felt kind of good. Destructive . . .

I wiped the sweat off my face and checked my watch. Just a little over an hour. And three strands of loose wire were laid on the ground. Nothing to it. Now all I had to do was roll them up.

I picked up the end of one strand and started to bend it into a circle. It was slow work bare-handed, but if I was real careful . . . I was almost through the fourth loop. Looking good. Neat. No loose ends. I let go with my right hand to start adding another loop. All of a sudden the whole coil sprang apart. Wire whipped in all directions, the barbs ripping through the air like angry wasps. One snagged my jacket while another drew blood on the back of my hand, but it was the sudden sting on my left cheekbone that got my attention. I reached up and touched the spot and my finger came away red. The cut was nothing, but the barb had missed my eye by less than half an inch. Laura's voice replayed in my mind. "This stuff can be dangerous." I was beginning to understand.

I started over. This time I thought about what I was doing. Weave it in and out, Laura had said. Okay. I started to catch on. It really did work. But you had to hold onto the roll. Tight. And the heavier that roll got, the harder it got to hold on without grabbing any barbs, like trying to squeeze a porcupine without squeezing any quills.

At first I noticed every cut. Stopped, sucked the blood off and tried to make it quit bleeding before I picked the wire up again. But after a while it didn't matter. I couldn't see the new cuts because of the blood from the old ones. I just kept rolling wire, and stopping every few feet to unsnarl the three wires when they'd got all crossed up with each other. I should have done it one wire at a time — like Laura said.

Yeah, sure, everything had to be like Laura said, I thought furiously. Well, not this time. I'd get it done. I'd show her.

I didn't think I'd ever finish that first roll. I wasn't even half done when it go so heavy all I could do was roll it along the ground to wind more wire on. Finally I cut the wire and started a new roll. I didn't know how Laura would like that — and I didn't care.

At last I was finished with the first wire. I flopped down in the mosquito-filled shade and just lay there, too tired to move for a few minutes. But then I got up. In my mind, I could see Laura driving over the hill any minute now, taking over and finishing my job, with that know-it-all look on her face. I started the middle wire.

By now my hands were so sore I didn't even feel the new cuts, and the fronts of my jean legs were stained red-black from wiping blood on them, but I didn't care. I was going to get this done.

The second wire seemed a little easier than the first. There was only one other loose wire for it to tangle with, and maybe I was getting a little smarter. But not smart enough to quit. My back was aching so bad from bending over and rolling the heavy coils of wire I could hardly straighten up. I figured if I ever stopped moving I'd stiffen up real fast. So I didn't stop. There was no breeze here in the thick woods and the afternoon sun was turning this place into an oven. Before I started on the last wire I threw my jacket over a post. The mosquitoes had a party but I was too tired to care. Roll, weave, lift, untangle, cut, bleed.

I leaned the last big coil of wire against a post. I leaned against it, too. It was about all that was keeping me from falling over. My back muscles were quivering and I was breathing like I'd just run the marathon. All I wanted to do was collapse on the soft grass and bury my throbbing hands in the cool mud. I felt like I was going to be sick. But I was done.

"You hear that, Laura? I'm done!" I yelled the words into the silent forest. Yeah, I thought. I'm done and now *I'm* waitin' for *you*. What you waitin' for, Laura? I started to laugh — and almost ended up crying instead. Hey, take it easy, man. You're losin' it. Don't go getting lightheaded on me just because you haven't eaten for . . . For the first time in hours, I looked at my watch. I stared blankly at the numbers, not believing what they said. Four-sixteen. It couldn't be. I'd been working on this all day? But what had happened to Laura and Ty? They should have been back hours ago.

I hadn't even finished that thought when I heard the sound of the motor. Wearily, I raised my head. A truck was coming down the fence line but for a second I wasn't sure it was Laura's truck. It hardly looked like a truck at all. More like some prehistoric monster just risen from the slime pits. Every bit of the body and most of the roof were covered in gooey black mud. Even the windows were so splattered I couldn't see inside. Only the space cleared by the windshield wipers shone through.

The truck stopped. It was Laura's, all right. Casually, I slid my hands behind my back, out of sight. Ty jumped out.

"Hey, Dare," he yelled, "you should have been there. Man, did we get stuck! Laura tried to drive through this mudhole and she *buried* the truck! We had to walk all the way over to the Godwins' and borrow their tractor. Laura said it was closer than home. And then we got that stuck, too." Ty kept on going but I was only half listening. Mostly, I was looking at Laura. She had gotten out of the truck and was standing there staring down the fence line. Then her eyes came back to survey me. I met her stare.

Eat your heart out, Laura, I thought. The job's done. You got nothin' to rag at me about. I didn't say that, though. Instead I gave the truck a meaningful glance. "Forget it was a four by four, not a tank, Laura?" I asked innocently.

I watched as her face started to turn red. No kiddin'. Laura blushed. It was the first time I'd ever seen her embarrassed. It was also the best moment I'd had all day. But I wasn't done with her yet. Before she had time to say anything I forced myself to stand up straight and move away from the post I'd been leaning on. "Where do you want the wire?" I asked, real laid back, like I rolled up a few miles of wire before breakfast every day.

Laura hesitated. "Okay," she said, just as casually, "let's get it in the truck. Come on, Ty. Give us a hand."

The coils were heavy, even for the three of us. I tried to keep my bloodied hands out of Laura's sight but it wasn't any use. She noticed. I felt her staring at them as we lifted up the first coil but I wouldn't meet her eyes and she didn't say anything. But Ty did, of course. I heard him give kind of a gasp.

"Dare, what did you do to your . . ." he began.

"Shut up, Ty," I said dangerously.

We loaded the last coil and got in the truck. Laura gunned it toward home. It was a pretty quiet trip.

We were almost there when Laura shot me a sideways glance. "If you were working for me, Dare, I'd fire you for pulling anything so stupid."

I shot a look back at her. "If I was working for you, Laura, I'd have quit a long time ago. Besides, I got the job done. How I got it done is none of your business."

Laura gave a disgusted snort. "When you leave bloody fingerprints all over my door handles, it's my business," she said gruffly. So much for Laura's brand of sympathy.

As soon as we walked into the house, Laura threw three T-bones under the broiler. "I'll have mine rare," Ty announced, automatically starting to set the table. "I could eat a whole cow, couldn't you, Dare?" he asked, already forgetting he was mad at me.

I shook my head, "I'm not hungry, I'm goin' to bed." I wasn't feeling real great.

"No, you don't." Laura's commanding voice stopped me.

I stared at her. "What?"

"You go wash those hands and then get yourself back out here. As soon as we eat I'm taking you into town for a tetanus shot. With all those wire cuts you're a prime candidate."

"Had one last month at school," I said. I hated needles. I'd almost skipped out to avoid that one. Now I was real pleased that I didn't.

Laura looked pleased, too. "Good, that'll save a trip."

"*Now* can I just go to bed?"

"No. Now I'm going to clean those cuts up for you."

"Oh no you're not."

Laura shrugged. "Okay. I guess we go to town after all. The doctor'll do a better job anyway. Probably put you in the hospital overnight."

I sighed. Trying to outmaneuver Laura was like trying to arm wrestle an octopus. I washed. We ate. Somewhere in there I discovered I was hungry after all.

Then Laura got out a pan of warm water and a big bottle of antiseptic. Even the *smell* of that stuff hurt. She poured about half the bottle in the water. Then she set the pan in front of me. I wasn't going to like this.

"Okay, Dare," she said pleasantly, "soak 'em."

Ty sat down at the end of the table, looking like he was about to witness open-heart surgery. "Bet that's really gonna hurt, Dare," he said, looking more interested than sympathetic.

I scowled at Laura. It didn't impress her. "Okay, okay," I growled. "This oughta make your day."

"Probably will," she said calmly.

I stuck my hands in the water. Ty was right. It hurt so much I almost jerked them out again. But I didn't. By now my pride had got involved. I looked up at Laura and grinned. "You sure this is strong enough?" I asked.

She gave me a dangerous look and then she started to reach for the bottle again.

"Just kiddin'," I said, backing off fast.

"You'd make a lousy poker player," Laura said, and started washing dishes, leaving me to soak and sweat.

She finally came back and let me out of the water. She studied my hands and shook her head. "You're a mess, Dare," she said, sounding disgusted. I hated to admit it, but for once in her life, she was right. I kept my mouth shut as she spread some kind of salve all over my palms and then wrapped the whole mess up in gauze so I looked like Rocky just ready to put on his gloves. She muttered and grumped the whole time about stupid kids. Being at her mercy like that, I just sat there and took it. I did notice, though, that for being so mad at me, she was pretty gentle about her doctoring.

She finally finished tying up the last bandage. Then she stepped back and looked me over. "Okay, hotshot," she said, "how do you feel?"

I looked up at her. "I'll live."

She nodded. "No doubt. Only the good die young." Her voice was grumpy as usual but something close to a grin crept across her face as she turned away.

I lay awake a long time that night, thinking about how I could learn to hate Laura McConnell.

Chapter 14

The next week was pretty calm. I didn't have much choice about that. My hands were so sore for a couple of days that even eating was hardly worth the pain. But there was still a good side. I definitely couldn't wash dishes. That must have broken Laura's heart. She and I were getting along kind of funny ever since the barbed-wire business. I knew that in one way she was furious at me for the whole thing, but I also think I'd gained kind of a grudging respect for calling her bluff.

Toward the end of the week, I was feeling pretty good again. Real good, come to think of it. Saturday night was the AC/DC concert in Calgary and I was going. How I was going needed a little figuring. After the Pits party I didn't think asking Laura if I could go was a real good idea.

Then, Wednesday evening, I got the perfect solution — from Laura herself. At supper she announced she was going to a Quarter Horse Association meeting in Red Deer on Saturday evening and not to wait up for her because she'd be real late. So would I.

Laura was meeting a friend up there for supper so she was out of the way in plenty of time. Ty watched disapprovingly as I got dressed. "Laura's not gonna like it," he said, like he was telling me something I hadn't heard before.

I stuffed my T-shirt into my jeans and pulled on my leather jacket. "Laura ain't even gonna know I've been gone."

"Wanna bet?" Ty said. "Last time you tried sneaking out it didn't work."

I turned to face him. "It didn't work because my brain-absent brother had to keep the mosquitoes out. It'll work this time if you cover for me," I said, cooling down.

"Lie for you, you mean," he shot back accusingly.

"Ty," I said wearily, "the only reason I'm still at Laura's is you."

It was dirty fighting but it worked. Ty's face turned red. "Okay, Dare," he said, staring at the door. "I won't tell on you."

"Promise?"

He looked up. "Yeah, I promise."

"Thanks, kid," I said, messing up his hair as I went outside to meet Keith.

I stepped out the door and saw Keith standing there with his hand out. For a second I thought he'd flipped out. "Let's have the money, man," he demanded, and suddenly I clued in. Automatically, my hand reached toward my pocket, and then froze in midair. Because I knew that the twenty-five dollars wasn't there anymore. I'd done a real good job of blanking out everything about Gran's funeral, all right. So good that one of the things I'd blanked out was giving Ty the concert money for flowers. Now, if I didn't think of something real fast, there wasn't going to be any concert.

"Come on, man, move it," Keith yelled over the rumble of the idling bike. "We ain't got all night."

"Yeah, yeah, I'm comin'. Just hang on a second." I turned and went back inside.

"Forget something?" Ty asked.

"Uh, yeah. My comb. Go see if it's in the top drawer of the dresser, will ya?"

Ty gave me a weird look, but he went. I figured finding the comb would take him a while — since I had it in my pocket. I should have time.

A second later I was kneeling on top of the kitchen counter, reaching behind the bowls on the top shelf. My hand touched the jar. I brought it out and sighed with relief. The money was still in it. Just like the day Laura had showed it to me. She and Ty were going fencing again but my hands were still healing so I was staying home. "The farrier said he might get time to come by and shoe Chance and Chief today," she'd said, reaching up into the cupboard and bringing out the jar. "If he does, pay him from the emergency money."

Well the farrier hadn't come, so I hadn't needed the emergency money that day. But today *was* an emergency. I dumped the money out. Over a hundred bucks. Enough to go a long ways. I stood there staring at it for a minute, thinking. No. I couldn't do that. Slowly, I unrolled two tens and a five and put the rest back. I was just closing the cupboard door when Tyler came back.

"I couldn't find it," he said. "Here, if you need a comb so bad, take mine." He held it out. I hesitated, starting to feel really lousy and wondering why. I took it.

"Thanks," I muttered, without meeting his eyes, and headed for the door.

I climbed on behind Keith. "Here's your stinkin' money," I said, jamming it into his hand. I was mad at him all the way to Calgary but I didn't know why.

Then we were at the Saddledome, moving through the doors in a sea of denim and leather and nothing else mattered except being a part of that restless and rowdy crowd. It was what I'd been wanting so bad. Freedom. A chance to lose myself in the sound and light and leave everything else behind. From the second that the band hit the stage and the first guitar notes screamed out of the big amps, the rest of the world was gone, blown away by the pounding beat. This was it. All there was. One huge, explosive carnival of light and fire and music where no one cared who you were or what you'd done. A legal high that was over too soon. I walked out of there so wired I felt like I could do anything, go anywhere, be anybody.

And it seemed like even nature wanted in on the

action. A thunderstorm was brewing over the city. Lightning was flashing and thunder was crashing close enough to make the pavement vibrate underfoot. But the storm didn't scare me any. I like storms. This one was just the grand finale to the concert. A crazy drum solo and the highest-voltage light show in the world.

"Come on, Keith," I said as we put our helmets on, "let me drive, huh?"

Keith scowled. "No way," he said. I could see he was still burned over the Pits.

I hung in there. "You drove down," I said. "Let me drive just halfway." I wore him down. He mumbled something and finally threw the key at me.

"Okay then, drive. But get goin'. It's gonna rain."

That was all I needed to hear. I *drove*, red-lining it all the way, speed shifting as I roared through the heavy traffic, laughing as I left fast cars behind.

We made it out of the city ahead of the storm and were cruising out toward Airdrie when I felt the first vibration. I thought I imagined it at first but it came again. All of a sudden I felt the bike slip into neutral. I tried to pull it out again. I couldn't. I eased over onto the shoulder and let it roll to a stop.

"What's the matter?" Keith yelled in my ear.

I cut the engine. "I don't know. Transmission, I think."

"Transmission?" Keith squawked. "You just tore the transmission out of my bike?"

"Me? I didn't do nothin'. I was just drivin' — "

"Yeah, maybe right now you were but you had to go and show off down at the Pits with it and you were drivin' the guts out of it in the city. Now what are we gonna do?"

"Hitchhike home, I guess."

"Oh, sure. That sounds like one of your ideas. Hitchhike home and leave my bike on the highway to get ripped off."

"You got any better ideas?"

He thought a minute. "Yeah. We're a lot closer to Calgary. We'll hide the bike in the ditch and catch a ride down to my dad's place. He'll bring his truck and pick it up."

I sighed. It was going to be a long night. Laura was going to get home first. Have a flat tire or something, Laura, please.

Chapter 15

Hitchhiking on Number Two at midnight is a real interesting experience — in the same way that playing Russian roulette is interesting. Every car that doesn't get you is sort of a victory. Because it seems like every one of them is aiming straight for you. I think half the drivers have seen too many movies like *The Hitcher* and they figure that anybody trying to get a ride is a homicidal maniac and fair game for target practice.

The other half don't even see you. They just come barreling down that highway with their lights on bright and their eyes shut tight and if they happen to pick you off with the outside mirror, too bad.

There are two ways to go about trying to hitch a ride. One is to be careful. Stand well back — with one foot in the ditch is good — and make sure you don't get hit. You also don't get noticed. We tried it that way for the first half hour.

Then another thunderstorm was getting close so we tried the second way and got aggressive. Lean right out into traffic so the headlights are sure to pick you up. That way there's a good chance you *will* get hit — but you still don't get a ride.

Car after car whizzed by, close enough to touch.

"Forget it, Dare," Keith gasped at last as we stood breathing in the fragrance of the double-decker load of pigs that had just rumbled past us. "We might as well just lie down in the ditch and wait till daylight. We're not gonna get a ride tonight."

"Sure, that's a cool idea, Keith. Ditches are a lot of fun in rainstorms. They get full of water and — "

"Oh, shut up, Dare. You've always got all the answers. Well, if you hadn't ratched the bike we wouldn't be in this mess. I'd rather be wet and alive than end up gettin' trashed by one of these maniacs."

"Yeah? Well, it don't matter when *you* get home 'cause your old lady lets you get away with murder. If Laura finds out I'm gone she'll eat me alive."

"So that's it. Laura again. You know, ever since you've been at her place you've been scared to sneeze in case she finds out. You know what I think? You're goin' soft, Dare. You're turnin' into Laura's good little boy, just like your wimp of a kid brother."

I almost decked him right then. I had my fist clenched ready. But then I spotted the car. It was a slow one. This one was going to stop.

I pushed Keith out of my way. "Look out, Ericsson," I said through my teeth. "This is my ride and if you want to share it shut your mouth."

The car had a burned-out headlight and the other one was on bright. It blinded me enough that it took me a second to decide which side the dead one was on. The far side. It had to be because the good one was so close to the right side of the lane. I stepped out so the driver could get a good look at me — and almost got turned into a hood ornament. I was already diving headfirst for the ditch by the time my brain caught up to my reflexes. The good headlight had been on the *left* side of the car. The idiot behind the wheel was taking the scenic route, straight down the shoulder.

I hit the ditch cussing and barely avoided doing a face stand in the gravel.

I was just sitting up to check the damage when Keith grabbed me by the jacket collar and dragged me to my feet. "Hey, come on, man. Let's go! The guy stopped."

Before I could answer he was gone, pounding up the highway toward the taillights of the waiting car. Great, Keith, I thought, just great. The guy practically kills me and you can't wait to meet him. He probably only stopped so he could come back and take another run at me.

"Okay, okay, I'm comin'," I yelled, breaking into a reluctant jog.

When I got close enough to see the car — well, actually it was a van — I almost burst out laughing. The dead headlight should have given me a clue. The whole thing was dead. It just hadn't made it to the junkyard yet.

It was a Chevy, a '72, '73, maybe — when cars get as old as I am I'm not too accurate at picking the years — and it was dark blue. Or at least it had been dark blue. Now it looked more like a pinto horse than anything else. Dark blue with big splotches of oxy-red primer blotched all over it. Still, I thought sarcastically, it *was* a real hotrod van. I mean, it had mags, didn't it? Chrome mags. Rusty chrome mags. Awesome.

Hey, Dare, I reminded myself. It's got wheels. It's headed for Calgary. And it's raining out here.

Right then the driver's side door swung open, kind of drunkenly. There was something wrong with the hinge. Then the driver got out, even more drunkenly, and I got my first view, not to mention smell, of our new buddy. The looks took a few minutes to absorb but the smell was instantaneous — brewery, with a good whiff of unwashed body thrown in.

The guy was about six-two with a big nose and a long neck and an Adam's apple that just wouldn't quit. More than anything else he reminded me of an undernourished chicken but, from the looks of his hair, all grease and sideburns, he must have figured he was Elvis Presley. He gave me a bleary-eyed look and then grinned a yellow grin.

"Howdy," he said.

No kiddin'. That's really what he said. It was about then that I noticed he was wearing a satin cowboy shirt — with fringes, yet — and a belt with a fake silver buckle big enough to do him some permanent damage if he happened to bend over too fast. Yup, what we had here was one genuine imitation cowboy.

"Shooter's the name," he said, "and partyin's my game." He laughed like a jackass and gave me a slap on the shoulder that almost knocked me over. "What'd you hit the ditch for, boy? You oughta trust ol' Shooter." That must have been the funniest thing he'd said all year because he leaned over and gave me a poke in the ribs, let go another bray of laughter and practically knocked me out with a faceful of secondhand beer fumes.

I stood there staring at him like he was a hallucination or something, but he didn't seem to notice. He just kept on with his comedy routine. "What are you boys doin' out in the middle of the night, anyway? Your girlfriends steal your car?" Another laugh and another jab in the ribs. If this kept up I was going to need medical attention.

Keith spoke up. "My motorcycle's back there in the ditch," he said sourly, making sure to give me a dirty look. "The transmission's ratched."

Shooter scratched his chin thoughtfully. "Motorcycle? You fellas don't belong to them Hell's Angels or somethin', do you?" he asked suspiciously.

"Not exactly."

"Oh," he said, looking a little disappointed. He gawked at us a while longer and thought some more. I was ready to start walking again by the time he finally made up his mind.

"Well," he drawled, "I guess you ain't likely to give us any trouble me and Ronnie can't handle.

Pile in back there." He stepped back so we could get in through the driver's door. "You gotta crawl in from here," he explained. "The back door don't work."

I hesitated. Getting out of the rain was one thing. Getting tied up with this guy was something else. But Keith nudged me impatiently. "Hurry up before he changes his mind. It's starting to rain harder." I climbed inside.

A shorter guy with a bald head and a big fluffy mustache eyed us blearily from the passenger side. "That there's Ronnie," Shooter announced. Ronnie nodded solemnly and popped the top of a can of beer. He didn't seem too thrilled to see us. That made the feeling mutual as far as I was concerned. This whole deal was starting to give me bad vibes. I wished I was back in the rain. But it was too late now. Shooter was peeling back onto the highway.

"Didn't catch you fellas' names," he said, tromping on the gas pedal and turning around to stare at us. We told him — first names, that is — and that seemed to satisfy him. He turned around and swerved just in time to avoid taking out the guard-rail on a curve he almost missed. That seemed to smarten him up a little. He kept his eyes on the road for a while, and I relaxed enough to take a look around me.

One thing for sure, the inside of the van had as much class as the outside. In the front the two captain's seats were so tattered they looked like they'd been salvaged from a junkyard. The dim, dust-filtered light that glowed from the instrument panel gave the cracked top of the dash an interesting effect. It had as many canyons as an aerial view of the Rocky Mountains. Somebody had tried a do-it-yourself job of customizing the walls, which made it real cozy in there — especially if you like warped particle board hanging over you shedding passion purple shag rug into your hair.

But the one thing that really caught my eye was the gun rack, sagging dangerously from one warped wall. There were two high-powered rifles and a shotgun in it and *they* looked shiny and well-used. That fact worried me for a minute, but then I decided that these guys were too dumb to be dangerous. More likely just a pair of those if-it-moves-shoot-it-type of hunters that cruise the back roads year-round trying to find something to kill.

Traffic had thinned out a lot by now, which was a good thing, since Shooter used all three lanes and the shoulder most of the time. Getting in here was a big mistake. When we hit the city I was getting out, fast. We were coming up to the Sixteenth Avenue turnoff when Shooter turned around — he *always* turned around to talk. "So, where you boys wanna go?" he asked between gulps from the can of beer he was working on.

"Look out!" Ronnie squeaked and Shooter remembered he was driving just in time to miss putting us in the back of a cattle truck. Keith told him the address. "It's way out in southwest," Keith said. "I can show you how to get there."

"No problem." Shooter giggled happily — and wheeled the van into the next exit. It happened to be the one for Sixteenth Avenue *east*. If this was going to get us to southwest Calgary, Shooter knew something I didn't know. I was getting out of here. Like right now, when we stopped for the light that had just flashed red at the next intersection. I had turned to tell Keith when that old engine gave a shudder and a howl of pain and a burst of speed threw me back against the seat. "Hey!" I squawked, "watch it, Shooter! You just ran a red light doin' sixty miles an hour."

He looked back with a grin. "You bet. Ya gotta go through them suckers fast. If you go slow somebody might hit ya." He pitched his empty can out the window. "Gimme another brew, Ronnie."

Ronnie rummaged in the case between the seats. "All gone," he said sorrowfully.

"Aw, no, that can't be. We gotta get some more."

"Too late," Ronnie said. "Everything's closed."

Shooter suddenly laughed and made a screeching turn into a side street. "Well, we'll just solve that problem," he said. "We'll get some from Uncle Don." He pulled to a stop in an alley behind some sort of shopping center.

"Oh, no," Ronnie argued. "I'm not gonna try that again."

"What's the matter with you, boy? Where's your guts?" Shooter snarled at him. "If I gotta do this alone, next time you're not comin', understand?"

Ronnie cowered in the seat, looking embarrassed

and small. It seemed like crossing Shooter scared him more than facing up to Uncle Don, whoever he was.

"Well?" Shooter growled.

"I'm comin'," Ronnie whined.

"You boys just wait," Shooter ordered. "This won't take long." He lurched out the door and Ronnie crawled across the seat and followed him. It seemed like that was the only door in the whole van that actually worked. Shooter slammed it behind them and they disappeared around the corner of a building in the pouring rain.

Keith looked at me. "What was all that about?" he asked. "Where'd they go?"

I shrugged. "Who knows? Come on, get that door open and let's get out of here before those hillbillies come back."

Keith gave me a blank look. "Are you outa your mind, Jamieson? It's pouring out there, it's two A.M., we're twenty miles across the city from my dad's place and I've got fifty-five cents in my pocket. What are we gonna do — walk or call a cab?"

"Hey, man, I don't know what we're gonna do but I'm not stayin' here. These guys are so drunk they can't see straight, and even sober I doubt that either one of their brains is hittin' on all eight cylinders. If you're not gettin' out, I am." I pushed past him and reached for the door handle. I tried to turn it. It didn't turn. Swearing, I jiggled it back and forth. It had to work. Shooter had got it open. There was a click . . .

A flash of movement under the streetlight caught my eye. Shooter and Ronnie were coming toward us at a dead run.

Next thing I knew the half-open door was jerked open wide and I was knocked back into Keith's lap as Ronnie and Shooter piled in. Shooter started the engine and slammed it into reverse.

"I told you so," Ronnie was growling, "you and your bright ideas — "

"Aw, shut up," Shooter cut him off as he burned out into the street. "How was I supposed to know there was an automatic alarm?"

We went around the corner on two wheels and for the first time I saw the front of the building we'd been parked behind. It was a liquor store — and it had a big hole in the front window.

I almost started banging my head on the wall. Talk about my brother being innocent. How could I have missed cluing in? Uncle Don? Don Getty, the premier of Alberta. These idiots had just tried to knock over an Alberta government liquor store. And I'd just sat there arguing with Keith until I missed my chance to get out.

I heard sirens in the distance. Shooter must have heard them, too. He swore and sped up. He went around a lot of corners and down some side streets and I didn't know where we were. At least these streets are pretty well empty at this time of night, I thought, as we squealed around a corner on the wrong side of the road — and came face to face with a street-sweeping machine. This is it, I thought, burying my head and getting ready for the crash.

But it didn't come. The van swerved wildly and when I looked up I was almost cheek to cheek with a mannequin in a passing store window. We were driving down the sidewalk, clipping off parking meters like a swather going through a grain field. Ronnie was swearing at Shooter at the top of his voice, Keith was screaming something and Shooter was yelling back at both of them. I wasn't saying anything. The more scared I get the quieter I get — and this was about the quietest I'd ever been.

Shooter got the van on the street again. Another intersection. Another red light. Shooter ripped right on through. Suddenly, a cop car shot out of a parking lot right behind us, party lights flashing and siren screaming. Shooter floored it.

This isn't real, I thought, as we roared through the sleeping city with the cop car on our tail. This isn't happening. I'm sitting in the theater watching *Beverly Hills Cop* or something and my imagination's getting away on me. Shooter screeched around another corner and sideswiped a parked car. He still didn't slow down but the jolt told me it was real all right.

I wanted to grab old Shooter by his overactive Adam's apple, toss him out of the way and pull over before we ended up smeared all over. We made another turn and the street sign caught my eye — Blackfoot Trail. But then I thought about the cops.

After this little performance they weren't going to hand Shooter a thirty-dollar ticket and send us home. He was — no, *we* were — in real deep.

The tires squealed and we rocked through another turn. I tried to see where we were. Going up onto an overpass. Another sign. SLIPPERY WHEN WET. Great, I thought. And it's raining cats and dogs out.

The first skid cut that thought short. Then the rear end was fishtailing, out of control. It felt like we were flying. I could see the lights of the city spread out below. Beer cans were whizzing around the inside of the van like missiles. I ducked, there was a huge crash and everything went blank.

Chapter 16

I opened my eyes and wondered why all the street-lights were upside down. Then it dawned on me that *we* were upside down. Cautiously, almost afraid to try to move in case I couldn't, I started trying to untangle myself. Surprisingly enough, I seemed to be okay.

I glanced over at Keith. He was huddled up in a heap, mopping at a bloody nose with his sleeve and muttering to himself. Outside of his nose, he didn't look in too bad shape. Up front, Ronnie was cradling an arm that looked broken and swearing a blue streak at Shooter for getting him into this mess. He was wasting his breath. Shooter was unconscious.

But somewhere I could hear a high-pitched screaming. Somebody must be hurt real bad. I turned my head, trying to see who it could be, and saw a flash of blue light instead. Then a red flash. There were red and blue lights all over the place. Suddenly, I clued in. The screaming was a siren. There were cop cars out there.

"All right, if you can hear me in there, come out

with your hands up." The amplified voice boomed into the van. The cops weren't taking any chances on tangling with us at close range. Man, we were one dangerous bunch of dudes, I thought. The whole idea would have been funny if I hadn't been stuck right in the middle of this whole mess. And then the full impact of that thought hit me. We *were* in a mess, all right. In Shooter's van, with two attempted robbery suspects, and — I glanced sickly at the bent rifle rack on the wall — a bigger arsenal than Rambo had used to wipe out half the Russian army. Man, were the cops going to love this setup. They were going to drag us all down to the station and ask questions and when they found out we were juveniles they were going to phone home and . . .

Oh, no. Not that. They weren't going to phone Laura and get her down here in the middle of the night to explain how I just happened to be out knocking over liquor stores when she thought I was home in bed. There had to be another way.

I nudged Keith. "Hey," I said in a desperate whisper, "if they ask you who I am don't tell 'em." He looked at me like I'd lost my mind but my thoughts were running on ahead, figuring it all out. It would work. I didn't have any ID on me. They couldn't find out who I was if I didn't tell them. And if they didn't know, they couldn't phone my guardian. Laura wouldn't find out. And right now that was all that mattered. I'd get this whole mess straightened out eventually — and then I'd decide if I'd go back or not.

"I repeat, come out with your hands up. Come out now." The voice was getting an edge to it. Like the guy with the megaphone was getting mad — or nervous. Maybe he figured we were getting ready to come out blasting away and he was going to shoot first and ask questions later.

I reached past Keith, who couldn't seem to get his mind past his ruined nose, and gave the door handle a jerk. It worked better upside down. The door rasped open about a foot. "Come on, Ericsson. Let's get outa here," I said, trying to get him to lead, follow, or at least get out of my way.

"Leave me alone," Keith mumbled, tenderly pressing his sleeve against his nose and glaring at me like this whole thing was my fault.

I gave up and crawled over top of him and started easing myself out the door. "Remember," I warned him over my shoulder, "you don't know me."

"I wish."

I stumbled out into the blinding glare of a spotlight. I stood there, too dazed to move, feeling like a jacklighted deer and wondering nervously when the hunter was going to blow me away. Suddenly a figure stepped into the light beside me and a hand grabbed my shoulder, spinning me around and slamming me against the side of the van.

"Get your hands on the van and don't move," a voice barked in my ear. Too stunned to do anything else, I obeyed. Hands roamed over my body. Looking for what, I wondered. Deadly weapons? Sorry, guys, I didn't bring my M-16 on this mission.

The cop finished his search. Okay. Satisfied? Now you can let me go. That thought was only half finished when he suddenly grabbed my arm and twisted it behind my back. I felt cold steel bite into my wrist. He jerked the other arm back, there was a click and I was wearing a pair of handcuffs.

Instantly my temper exploded. I turned on the cop. "Hey, you can't — " He grabbed my shoulder and bounced me off the side of the van, hard enough to get my attention. Then before I could even get my wind back he started reciting a speech at me.

"You are under arrest for breaking and entering and theft. Do you wish to say anything? You are not obliged to do so but whatever you say may be given as evidence. Do you understand?"

I turned my head and stared at him. "Breaking and entering? Theft? Hey, you've got it all wrong. I didn't — "

"Do you understand?" he repeated.

"Okay, okay, I understand, but I still didn't — "

He grabbed me roughly by the shoulder. "All right, let's go," he said, and then he and another cop were marching me off toward a waiting police car. I managed one last glance over my shoulder. Among the police cars were two or three ambulances. Shooter and Ronnie were being lifted onto stretchers and a couple of cops were walking Keith over to one of the ambulances. An ambulance for a broken nose? Ericsson, you wimp . . .

I watched the ambulances go screaming off and suddenly it dawned on me. Out of the four of us I was the only one who wasn't hurt. All the others were on their way to the hospital. But not me. I was lucky. I was going to the police station.

Fifteen minutes later I was sitting in this little room being hassled by the same jerk who arrested me. Corporal Matthews was his name.

"All right," he said, not even bothering to look up from the form he was filling out, "what's your name?"

I didn't say anything.

"Your name?" he repeated, impatiently. This time he did look up. I looked at the floor. He breathed a deep, disgusted sigh. "So we're gonna play games, huh, punk? Well, that's just fine. They *pay* me to sit around here all night so that's just what we're gonna do till you show a little cooperation. Now let's try again. What's your name?"

I was getting sick of this. Okay, so he wants a name. Give a name and make him happy. Joe Smith. That was the first one that popped into my mind. Come on, Dare, he'll never buy that. Think of something original . . .

All at once, I had it. "Angus Young." I blurted it out loud and clear just like I owned it. Then I realized where the name had come from and just about died. The concert. Angus Young. AC/DC's lead guitarist. Way to go, Dare. Nice, inconspicuous choice. Only about ten thousand people saw him tonight.

I looked up at the cop slowly, ready to duck if he decided to belt me for getting smart. But believe it or not, the guy was actually buying it. He was writing it down. I breathed a sigh of relief. Obviously, this wasn't an AC/DC fan. But then again, I didn't figure many cops were.

He looked up. "Okay, Angus," he said, and I had to cough to smother a grin, "keep it coming. Birth date?"

That one I could handle. The truth about my birthday couldn't do much harm. "July tenth," I said.

"Year?"

Whoa. Being fifteen was a bad idea. Fifteen-year-olds were supposed to have parents — parents the cops would phone. I did some fast math and aged three years in five seconds. "In 1970," I said.

Matthews looked up and studied me awhile. Come on, man, believe it. I looked him in the eye, daring him to call me a liar. He shrugged and wrote it down.

"Address?" The questions were getting tougher. It was my turn to shrug.

"No fixed address," I said, remembering hearing that phrase about some murder victim on the news. He wrote that down.

"Okay, Angus," he said, "do you have a statement to make?"

"Yeah. I didn't do nothin'. So when do I get out of this dump?"

Matthews gave me a dirty look. "With your attitude it could be a while," he said. He stood up. "Let's go."

"Where to?"

"The cell block."

"Hey, you can't — "

Matthews jerked me to my feet. "Yes, I can. You have been arrested for a crime that is still under investigation. You will be held here overnight until the other parties involved have been questioned." He marched me out and down a long hall. He really was going to lock me up. I hadn't counted on this. But I could handle it. I'd spent part of Halloween night in the Crossing jail last year. It was nothing.

Chapter 17

Matthews took me through a door and into a big room with a bunch of cells in it. It must be a busy night. They all looked full. I stared at the people inside. They looked back at me, not real interested. Just kind of vacant, like I was one more side of meat going through the packing plant.

The cop opened the cell at the far end and motioned me inside. I stepped in and he slammed the door shut, hard. Like it gave him a lot of satisfaction to hear the clang echo off the concrete walls. It had a real final sound — as if once that door closed it would never open again. A shiver ran through me. "Sleep tight, Angus," Matthews said sarcastically and walked away.

I turned to look around and suddenly the lights dimmed, leaving the cell partly in shadow. Bedtime at the zoo, I thought, and, right on cue, the gorilla eased himself up from a bunk. He was the biggest man I'd ever seen outside a wrestling ring. He must have weighed close to three hundred pounds. But as he came shuffling out of the shadows I forgot about his size. It was his hair I couldn't take my eyes off. It was red. Carrot red. And I'd never seen so much hair on one human being in my life. It hung almost to his waist and bushed out in all directions like a lion's mane.

He just stood there for a minute, peering at me through all that forest and grinning through a beard that matched. It was kind of a hollow grin. His four front teeth were missing.

Then he reached out and took hold of the bars with his huge hands. Automatically, my eyes followed the movement. He was wearing a jean jacket with the sleeves ripped out and his arms were bare — except for the tattoos. Big, complicated ones that looked like they'd been done by a real expert. A dagger on his left arm, complete with blood dripping off the end. But the one on the right was the real showstopper. A skull — with a real nice, healthy-looking set of teeth. I noticed the teeth because they were clamped down on the body of a girl who also looked pretty healthy for the situation she was in.

Slowly, the guy turned his massive head toward me. "Welcome to the real world," he rumbled from somewhere deep in his chest. I knew he was talking to me but his eyes never really focused. They didn't look at me. They looked through me, like he was seeing something a million miles beyond this place. Totally burnt, I thought. Not enough brain cells left to know which way is up.

I didn't say anything. The guy gave me the

137

creeps. He didn't say anything more but he stared down at his right arm. I followed his gaze. Suddenly, he flexed his bicep and that whole tattoo came to life. The skull seemed to twitch and grin and click those perfect teeth. I stared. I'd never seen anything like it before. He did it half a dozen times, like a dog showing off its best trick. Then, all of a sudden, he leaned his head real close to mine like he was going to tell me a secret and — honest to God — he *growled* at me. Just like a wild animal. I jumped like he'd bitten me and he threw back his head and laughed. The laugh was scarier than the growl. I started to back away — and almost bumped into another guy.

This one was huge, too. Did everybody over two hundred pounds automatically go to jail in this town? But there was a difference in the way they were big. The redhead was solid muscle. This one was soft, like he ran more to fat.

"You better look out for him," the new guy said in a real soft, almost whispery voice. "Animal's dangerous."

The fat guy went over to a bunk and sat down. "Come on over here, kid," he invited. He was smiling. He had enough teeth to make up for all the ones Animal was missing. But at least he didn't seem to be a growler. Hoping he didn't bite, either, I walked over.

"My name's Silk," he said, and already that purring whisper was getting on my nerves. I didn't tell him my name. By this time I wasn't so sure what it was, anyhow.

"First time in here?" he asked. I nodded. "It's tough until you know your way around," he said, smiling some more. The more he smiled the less I liked him. "Sit down," he said, moving over to make room for me. Silk gave me a long look. Too long.

"You know, kid, you've got to be real careful in a place like this. Guys like Animal around, you could get hurt. Understand what I'm saying?"

I wasn't exactly listening. I had just discovered the fourth guy in the cell. He was noisily rolfing his cookies in the general direction of the toilet in the corner. I leaned my head back against the wall and closed my eyes. If I had to get thrown in jail did it have to be with a psychotic ape, a drunk whose main activity was barfing on his boots and this over-stuffed used-car salesman who never shut up? The guy was still talking. I tuned in again. "You stick with me I can protect you from him."

Before I had time to sort that out, he had reached his big fat arm over and put it around my shoulders like he owned me or something. And right then I woke up. Protect me? Oh, sure, he'd protect me, all right. But who was going to protect me from *him*?

Shaking with a weird mixture of fear and fury, I jerked away from him and stood up, feeling like I'd just been touched by something slimy and poisonous. "Keep your hands off me, creep! Just stay away from me," I said hoarsely, starting to back away from him.

Silk heaved himself to his feet and his big soft face turned mean. "You shouldn't have done that, baby," he hissed. "I make a real good friend and a real bad enemy. Now I'm going to have to teach you some respect." He started coming toward me. I took another step back. And another. Then I felt the cold concrete wall against my back.

So fast I didn't even see it coming, Silk's big right hand came up and slapped me across the mouth so hard it snapped my head sideways. I tasted blood and felt it trickling warm from the corner of my mouth down my chin. In that second, a slow fuse began to burn in the back of my brain. Everything that had happened lately — Gran dying, all that stuff at school, Laura, getting mixed up with Shooter tonight — and now this.

I wiped my hand across my lip, stared at the blood on it for a second — and then exploded. I launched myself away from that wall like a fighting cat and lit into Silk with both fists. I went for his gut, his big soft gut — like the Pillsbury Dough Boy, I thought, smiling to myself as my fists sank into the flab. He was gonna pay for hitting me.

I got in three or four good punches and with every one I could feel him sort of deflate like a leaky balloon. For a couple of seconds there I really thought I was going to pound him into the floor.

But I hadn't figured on the sheer size of the guy. In spite of all that fat, he was strong. Suddenly he just locked his pudgy hands around my waist, picked me right up off my feet and threw me across the cell. My back hit the steel-barred door with a clang so loud that people outside on the street must have heard it. They probably heard me scream, too. It felt like every bone in my body snapped when I hit those bars. I bounced off, landed on the floor and lay there, limp. My mind was yelling at me to get up but my body refused to move.

Then it was too late. Silk's hands were closing around my throat and starting to squeeze. I tried to fight him off but my body still wouldn't respond. The world closed in to the size of a TV screen. Just Silk's gleaming snake eyes and those white hands on my throat.

"I'm going to kill you," the slippery voice whispered in my ear. The TV screen was getting smaller, starting to disappear into a warm red haze — and I knew that Silk was telling the truth.

Suddenly there was a roar that seemed to shake the cement walls. I caught one glimpse of red hair and tattooed arms.

"Leave him alone, Silk!" Animal bellowed as he launched his three hundred pounds at Silk. It was like two of Laura's range bulls colliding. Then they both hit the floor. Well, not exactly. I was between them and the floor. The impact tore Silk's hands off my throat — and knocked the little bit of breath I had left out of me. Right then the lights went out.

Dimly, like it was so far away that it didn't matter, I could still hear voices yelling threats and curses and there was a lot of crashing and slamming going on, but I was too spaced to relate to any of it. Just as long as I stayed in this safe darkness I'd be okay.

Then there were new voices, loud and full of authority, and gradually the yelling and slamming died down. I heard the cell door clanging open and then somebody was bending over me.

"Hey, Matthews," a voice called near my ear. "We better get this one outside and check him out. He could be really hurt." This one? Then my brain came into focus and I knew he meant me. It sounded like he was talking about a dog or a dead body. Couldn't he at least call me by name?

A hand touched my neck, feeling for a pulse. Oh, come on, guys, get serious. I may be shook up a little but I'm not dead. Then the hand moved to my shoulder and began to shake it. I recognized the style. Good old Matthews.

"Angus!" he said loudly. "Wake up, Angus." I opened my eyes and stared at him. What was this guy on, anyway? I'd been knocked out but he had flipped out. The only Angus I knew was Laura's black cow.

"What?" I mumbled dazedly, but all of a sudden the fog in my head cleared and I remembered. Angus! Of all the names in the world . . .

I groaned.

"Just take it easy, kid," another cop said, running his hands over me, to check for moving parts that didn't move, I guess. "Hurts, huh?"

"Yeah," I muttered. Waking up and realizing you'd just named yourself Angus hurt a whole lot.

This cop — Corporal Vinelli, his name tag said — finally decided I wasn't beyond temporary repairs, so he and Matthews dragged me out of the cell and sat me in a chair down in the office end of the room.

Vinelli took a first-aid kit out of a cupboard and started dabbing away at my bleeding lip with something that Laura would have liked. It stung real good.

I jerked my head away. "Leave me alone," I said, trying to sound tough and ending up sounding like I was going to bawl. Vinelli ignored me, took my chin in a firm hand and went on dabbing.

"How you feelin', kid, outside of the lip, I mean? Think you need a doctor?"

Impatiently I shook my head — and got my chin realigned for the second time. "No, I don't need a doctor," I said — which goes to show how stupid I am. If I'd have played dead a little I could have been in a nice safe hospital with Keith and his bloody nose. But of course I never thought of that till it was too late.

The cop finished playing medic, stuck a bandage across the corner of my mouth and turned my chin loose. Then he pulled up another chair and sat down.

"Okay, kid. What happened in there?" he asked, his voice gentle.

I looked at him. He was different from Matthews. He acted almost human. If I told him the truth, he just might believe it.

I took a deep breath and started to tell him. But the words never came out, because a sudden picture of Silk's cold eyes staring at me flashed across my mind. What if I told Vinelli and he gave Silk some static about it but then put me back in there again? Next time, Silk *would* kill me — especially if he found out I'd spilled my guts to the cops.

I stared at my fingernails. They were dirty. "Nothin'," I muttered.

There was a long silence. When I finally looked up, Vinelli shook his head. "Well, if that was nothing," he said wearily, "I sure hope I'm retired before *something* ever happens around here."

Then, before either of us could say anything else, Matthews was back. "Okay, Angus," he ordered, motioning for me to get up, "everything's under control again. Let's go." I stood up unsteadily.

Vinelli looked from Matthews to me and back to Matthews again. "You really gonna put him back in there?"

Matt shrugged. "What else? Seems like every bar in town's had a brawl tonight. Everything else is full. He's eighteen so there'll be hell to pay if we put him in with the juveniles. What do you want me to do with him, take him home and baby-sit him?"

Vinelli didn't waste an answer on that question.

He just shook his head, gave me one last searching look and walked away.

Matthews walked me back to the cell. "Here we are, Angus," he said with a nasty smile, "home sweet home." He took his time unlocking the cell. I stood there looking at the guys inside.

The drunk was throwing up again — he hadn't even made it to the toilet this time. Animal was leaning against the wall, his arms folded across his chest, staring into space. And Silk — Silk was sitting on the bunk, holding a paper towel to his nose, which was still oozing a little blood. He eyed me the way a hungry snake eyes a cornered rabbit.

I felt myself go cold and hollow inside. I couldn't go back in there. I had to get out of this place. Laura? No. Not Laura. I'd got myself into this. I had to get myself out. If you can't stand the heat stay out of the kitchen.

Matthews gave me an amused glance. "What's the matter, Angus?" he asked, mockingly. "You think of something you wanted to tell me?"

All of a sudden Corporal Steiger was no longer number one on my list of people I didn't want to be marooned on a desert island with. Matthews had him beat a thousand times over.

"Yeah." I spat the word at him furiously. "I've got lots of things I want to tell you. I want to tell you where you — "

Matthews's smile turned to a snarl. "Get in there, punk," he said, grabbing me by the shoulders and giving me a push. He was just pulling the door shut when a new cop came in.

"Hey, hang on a minute, Matthews," he said. "Is that the kid you were having trouble getting an ID on for that liquor store B and E?"

"Yeah," Matthews said, "what about it?"

"Got a lady out here described a missing juvenile. Sounded like it could be him." Suddenly my knees went weak, and I didn't know if it was from panic or relief. It couldn't be . . . could it?

"Got an ID on this one," Matthews said, his eyes on my face, watching for my reaction. "He's not a juvenile and his name's Angus Young."

"Oh. Okay," said the other cop. "Back to the drawing board, then." He turned to leave.

"My name's not Angus." The words just came out. I didn't mean to say them. "It's Darren Jamieson and I'm fifteen."

The cop checked a piece of paper. "Bingo," he said.

Chapter 18

We walked out into the real world where the people weren't in cages and there was Laura, pacing the floor like a captive cougar. Her back was to us but when she heard the door open she swung around to face us and right then I almost turned around and headed back to that cell. I'd never seen quite that expression on her face before. From the set of her jaw and the tense lines around her mouth I could tell she was plenty upset. I knew she was going to tear a strip a mile wide off me. I stared back at her defiantly. Okay Laura, just get it over with.

I took a deep breath and waited for her to start yelling. I wished my hands would stop shaking.

Then she was walking toward me. Was she really mad enough to hit me? I wondered, fighting the urge to take a step back. But all of a sudden, the hardness in her face dissolved. Before I knew what was happening she had her arms around me in a big, rib-crunching hug.

"Dare, are you all right?" she said in a worried whisper, still holding me tight. Nobody had held me like that for a long time. Not since . . .

"Yeah, I'm . . ." I started to say but I never got the words finished. Because that's when I realized I was crying. Dare Jamieson, the toughest kid in Crossing, standing in the middle of the Calgary police station, crying my guts out on Laura McConnell's shoulder in front of a bunch of cops. And I couldn't stop, either. It had been building up inside me for so long.

"It's okay, Dare. It's all over," Laura was saying, still holding me tight and rubbing my shoulder like I was a baby or a kitten or something. It felt so good.

Why didn't you just belt me one, Laura, I thought miserably, finally forcing myself to raise my head and break away. If you'd have hit me I wouldn't have cried.

"Come on, tough guy," Matthews broke in sarcastically, motioning toward an open office door. "You've still got a lot of explaining to do before you go home to your milk and cookies."

Thanks a lot, Laura, I thought bitterly, wiping my sleeve across my eyes and following her through the door.

The rest of what happened at the station is kind of a blur. Matthews kept us in there answering stupid questions for an hour or more. I don't even remember most of them. I know Laura showed him my birth certificate or whatever it took to get rid of Angus Young and get Dare Jamieson back. I answered still more questions — truthfully this time. Somebody had finally got around to questioning Ronnie and Shooter at the hospital and they backed up my story that Keith and I were just hitching a ride with them.

After that it seemed like Matthews had about run out of excuses to hassle me anymore. But he glanced over his notes one more time and when he looked up accusingly this time it was at Laura, not me.

"There's just one thing here that I don't quite understand, Ms. McConnell," he said officiously.

By this time Laura had her head propped up on her hand and she looked about as tired as I felt. "Oh," she said, "what's that?"

"Well, we have confirmed the fact that he and his friend were riding home from a rock concert here in the city on a motorcycle that broke down. Now, you, as his temporary legal guardian, actually gave permission for, uh, Darren — " he said my name suspiciously like he figured I'd shoplifted it somewhere " — a fifteen-year-old juvenile, to ride a motorcycle to a city seventy-five miles from your home and return after midnight along a busy highway?"

My stomach sank. Okay, I thought, that about cuts it. Now Laura tells him I went without permission, he starts checking with Social Services and I'm dead — or at least in a detention center. I looked at Laura but she wouldn't meet my eyes. I looked away.

"Why shouldn't I?" Laura said. "Dare's old enough to be responsible for what he does."

I just about fell off my chair. Laura, old straight-shootin' Laura, had just lied — well, maybe not in so many words, but the message Matthews got sure wasn't the truth — to save my neck.

Matthews gave her a disgusted look. "Well, Ms. McConnell," he said, "if that's your attitude as a guardian I just hope you're never put in charge of one of my kids."

Laura gave him her teacher look. "I certainly hope that, too, Officer Matthews," she said, poison-ously polite.

Matthews finally gave up. Ten minutes later Laura and I walked out into the cool night air.

I breathed in big gulps of it but I still couldn't get enough. I felt like taking off my clothes and diving into that clean, pure night like it was a pool of clear water and letting it wash away every trace of the inside of that jail.

I looked up at the gray sky. The rain had stopped and there was a thin silver sliver of moon up there. I felt like I could reach up and touch it if I really tried. I wanted to grab it and make sure it was real. To make sure I really was outside. That I wasn't dreaming and that I wouldn't wake up back behind those bars where the only moon was a light bulb that never slept.

I stood there a long time. Laura never said any-thing. She just waited. "Want to tell me about it, Dare?" she said at last.

I shook my head. "You don't want to hear it," I said.

"I probably don't," Laura said quietly and we started walking slowly across the parking lot toward the truck. But then I stopped again.

"Why'd you do it, Laura?"

Laura looked at me. "Do what?"

"You know. Come down here in the middle of the night and bail me out. Cover for me about sneakin' out tonight. I've been nothin' but trouble to you. Why didn't you just throw me to the wolves and get rid of me and get even all at once?"

Laura was quiet a long time. Finally she said, "I met a horse breeder from Montana at the meeting tonight. He'd seen Smoke when he was up this way a couple months ago and I guess he liked him, 'cause he offered me five thousand dollars to take that bad-mannered devil off my hands." She paused and then added, thoughtfully, "But I didn't sell old Smoke out, either."

I guessed I had my answer because Laura started walking again. "Come on," she said, "it's time your brother was home in bed."

"You brought Ty?" I asked, surprised.

Laura laughed. "He brought me is more like. Woke me up at two o'clock." She shook her head. "Poor kid was some worried."

I nodded, thinking guiltily of how I'd made Ty promise not to tell. The kid took promises real serious, too. Right then another thought hit me. "But how'd you know I was in jail? Ty didn't know that."

Laura laughed and shook her head. "About ten minutes after Ty told me where you'd gone I got an irate phone call from Mrs. Carol Ericsson — "

"Keith's mom phoned you to tell you where I was?"

"Not exactly. She phoned me to give me a piece of her mind — which heaven knows she can hardly spare," Laura added drily, "because I'd let you and your bad influence lead poor Keith into all sorts of trouble. She hollered at me for half an hour. Anyway, somewhere in there she mentioned that you were in jail where you belonged."

"You believe that? About me leading Keith astray?"

"I've had the pleasure of teaching Keith," Laura said with a crooked grin. For a non-answer it said a lot.

We were at the truck. The light from a streetlight shone on Ty's hair as he sat slumped against the passenger window, sound asleep. He looked so young, like an orphan or something, I thought. Brilliant, Dare. That's what he is. You're all the family he's got.

Laura opened the driver's door. "Get in this side. Maybe he won't wake up." I slid across the seat as quietly as I could but Ty raised his head. He rubbed his eyes and blinked like he wasn't sure where he was. Then he focused on me and his face lit up.

"Dare!" he said, but then as he looked me over the grin faded. I guess I was looking kind of rough. "What happened to you, anyhow?" he asked.

"It's a long story," Laura cut in, her voice gentle.

"He'll tell you some other time. Just go back to sleep, Tyler. It's a long ride home."

She started the truck and pulled into the quiet street. Tyler looked up at me. "Dare," he said softly, "I'm sorry. I couldn't help it. I had to tell. I was so worried."

I grinned at him and messed up his hair. "I understand, Ty. It's okay. I'm glad you did."

"You are?"

"Yeah."

Five minutes later he was asleep with his head on my shoulder. I wished I could go to sleep, too, but there was something else I had to settle — and I wasn't looking forward to it.

"Laura?"

"I'm listening."

"I owe you twenty-five dollars."

Silence.

"I, uh, took it out of the cupboard."

"Uh-huh."

"You already knew?"

No answer.

"I'll pay you back — if I ever get any money."

"Don't worry, I'll work it out of you."

Was that a threat or a promise? I decided it was both.

153

Chapter 19

I awoke to bright sunlight shining in my eyes. It must be late, I thought groggily, as I checked my watch. It said 10:18. Laura had let me sleep until 10:18. I looked over at Ty's bed. It was empty — and made, even. I started to sit up. Oh, man, was I sore.

And then I remembered last night. I wished I could forget it. Forget everything about it and pretend it had all been a bad dream. I closed my eyes again but that was a mistake. I could still see Silk, that evil grin gleaming in the darkness.

I gritted my teeth and dragged myself out of bed and over to the mirror to see if it was possible to look as bad as I felt. It was. My lip had swelled up and my eyes looked like I'd been on a two-week drunk. I hurt all over but my back seemed like it hurt the worst. I turned around and looked over my shoulder at it in the mirror.

Well, I sure hadn't dreamed the part about getting thrown across the cell. Three long, greenish-purple bruises angled across my shoulders, spaced the same distance apart as those bars had been. Pretty impressive — if you like looking like a zebra. Then it occurred to me that if the angle would have been just a little different I would have hit headfirst instead of back first. The picture of my brains redecorating the Calgary jail sobered me up real fast.

I finally got as far as the kitchen. Nobody home. I wondered what big project Ty and Laura had on today. I also wondered, kind of sheepishly, why Laura didn't have me out there working out her twenty-five dollars like she promised. She must be going soft, I thought. But I should have known better.

I was just pouring a cup of Laura's leftover poisonous coffee when Ty came charging in.

"Hey, Dare, about time you were up," he said, all bright-eyed and bushy-tailed, as he grabbed the milk out of the fridge and poured himself a glass. "Guess what?" he added, straddling a chair like he was about to break it to ride.

"What?" I asked cautiously.

"Laura and I just got Smoke corralled again. She's gonna trim his hoofs as soon as I get her gloves for her." He downed the milk in two gulps and headed for the door. "Aren't you comin' to see him?" he asked over his shoulder.

I just about said no. I didn't feel much like going anywhere to see anything and, after last night, I didn't want to face Laura for a year or two.

But curiosity got the better of me. After all I'd heard about Smoke, I had to see him close up. I doubted he was half the horse Ty always said he was — until I saw him, that is.

He came trotting across the corral, his neck arched, his black mane and tail flying like banners in the wind and his silver-blue hide gleaming like a polished gun barrel. I'd never seen anything so beautiful in my life. But it wasn't till an hour or so later that I knew I loved him.

I watched as he let Laura catch him. Let was the word for it, too. The way he stood there with his head high, his eyes looking past her to the fields beyond, I got the feeling that if Smoke ever decided he wasn't going to put up with something, he wouldn't.

As it turned out, he decided he wasn't about to put up with having his hoofs trimmed. It didn't start out too bad. Ty held the halter rope while Laura picked up his left front foot, held it between her knees and trimmed the uneven edges off with a big pair of clippers.

She was almost finished when, all of a sudden, a bunch of mares and colts came galloping up from the bottom of the pasture. That did it. Right then Smoke let out a loud whinny, reared straight up and jerked his foot out of Laura's grasp.

"Stop it, Smoke!" Laura ordered, giving him a slap on the belly with her open hand. "Never mind those other horses. You're paying attention to *me* now."

That was what Laura thought. Smoke thought something different. Every time she tried to finish that foot he'd jerk loose again and start edging closer to the fence so he could get a better look at those other horses. After about the fifth try, Laura got mad.

"Okay, Smoke, if that's the way you want it." She took a long piece of thick, soft rope and tied it loosely around his middle like a cinch. Then she made a loop and slipped it around his front foot and pulled the end of the rope up through the cinch rope. Smoke didn't have any choice. The foot came up and Laura tied it up. I had a feeling Smoke wasn't going to like this.

I was right. Seconds later, he whinnied, shifted impatiently and tried to put his foot down. Then all hell broke loose. He gave an infuriated squeal, roared, came down and fell on his knees. But that didn't stop him. Even on three legs he was up again instantly, fighting, squealing, falling again. Laura just stood back and watched calmly. I couldn't believe that. She was supposed to be so crazy over this horse.

After the fourth time he fell I turned on her angrily. "He's gonna kill himself!"

"Maybe," Laura said quietly.

"Well, then, why don't you — "

"Dare, there's something you better learn about horses. Old Smoke there has got fire and pride. That's what makes him a great horse, what'll keep him going after other horses have given up. He's also got a wild streak and a mean temper. That's what's going to make him a useless outlaw. Having his hoofs trimmed isn't hurting him and it isn't scaring him. He's fighting it out of pure orneriness. Until he gets that out of his system he's dangerous to himself and everyone around him. He'd be better off dead." She paused, pushed her hair out of her eyes and gave me a long, steady look. I turned away.

Smoke had finally stopped fighting. He stood, soaked with sweat, bleeding from a long scratch across one flank, trembling. Laura walked over to him. She rubbed his head gently.

"Ready to try again, Smoke?" she asked him in a soothing voice. He didn't move as she untied the rope from his foot. "Here, Dare." Laura handed the halter rope to me this time. I held it loosely, almost hoping that horse would unwind again. But he didn't. Laura trimmed the other three hoofs and he never even twitched.

At last she pulled off the halter, hand fed him a few mouthfuls of oats and let him go. For a minute he just stood there, watching her walk away. Then, all of a sudden, he ducked his head, gave a defiant squeal and made a couple of rounds of the corral, bucking and kicking and showing off for all he was worth. I saw Laura look back over her shoulder and laugh. I couldn't help laughing, too.

"Hang in there, Smoke!" I yelled. "Don't ever let her break you." Right then I knew that although I'd never own him, Doc's Smokin' Joe was my horse. We were two of a kind.

Chapter 20

For the next couple of days things were kind of quiet. Uneventful quiet, not lazy quiet. Laura kept us busy doing exciting stuff like repairing corrals and weeding the garden. I did what she told me. But I hated it. I hated it even more because I *owed* Laura. She had never said a word about that night in Calgary, and somehow I didn't think she ever would. But that didn't mean she'd forgotten it. And it sure didn't mean *I'd* ever forget it.

Then one morning I woke up to Ty shaking me and yelling in my ear.

"Come on, Dare, we've got to get goin'. Laura's already out getting the horses ready."

Reluctantly, I opened an eye. "Ready for what?"

"We're gonna brand today. Laura says it's past time to have it done and today's the day."

I yawned. "Brand what?"

"What d'ya think? Calves, of course. You know, round up all the cattle, separate the calves, rope 'em, throw 'em . . ."

Just hearing all this was making me tired. I opened the other eye. "Yippee," I said weakly.

Ty went right on. "And Laura says I can help her heel 'em."

I half sat up. "Why? Are they sick?" I asked, playing a little dumber than I really was just to bug my kid brother.

It worked. He rolled his eyes. "Dare," he said in that hopeless tone of voice I usually hear only from teachers, "you're never gonna make a cowboy."

"Aw, no, Ty," I said, real serious, "and bein' a cowboy was all I had to live for."

He finally figured out I was teasing him and threw a playful punch at me. He missed and landed sprawled out on the bed beside me. He propped himself up on one elbow and started carefully explaining to me like I was a real slow learner.

"Heeling is roping calves off a horse by their hind feet and stretchin' them out so the guys on the ground can brand 'em and stuff. It's real tricky. You gotta drop the loop where the calves gonna step in the next second. It takes a real good roper."

"Like you, huh?" I said, just to see his reaction. The first thing he did was start studying the floor like it was real interesting. But even though I couldn't see his face, I did notice his ears turning red. Finally, he looked up.

"Yeah," he said. "Laura says I'm not bad." To Ty, whatever Laura said was the way it was.

A minute later he was heading for the door. "Laura told me to tell you she's got a job for you, too," he said over his shoulder. "If you're up to it, that is."

If I was up to it. . . . Way to go, Laura, you've really got me figured, haven't you? Put it that way and I'd do it if I was dying. It looked like Laura was about to start collecting my dues. I sat up straight.

"You can tell Laura that, whatever it is, I'm up to it," I said. "What's she got lined up for me, anyhow? Following the cows around with a shovel to keep the corral neat?"

Ty threw me a cocky grin. "That'd be about your speed, Dare." He was gone before I could get my hands on him.

My first job was to help bring in all the cattle. Just the three of us. Laura had a bigger crew lined up to help with the branding but she said too many people just got the cows riled up when you were trying to corral them. Ty was riding Chance. I was stuck with the Chief, as usual, and when Laura came out of the barn she was leading Smokin' Joe himself, saddled and bridled.

"I didn't know he was broke to ride," I said.

Laura laughed. "He doesn't know it, either, but he's well enough started to be at least semi-controllable. The cows will teach him the rest."

This I had to see.

Well, the stallion was ridable, all right, if the rider happened to be Laura, who was just as stubborn and pigheaded as he was. Between the two of them they cut quite a swath through the brush as we combed the woods looking for cows. Once in a while they even managed to head a cow in the right direction, too, but Tyler and I did most of it. I finally found something the Chief could do right. He knew a lot more about chasing cows than I did — which sure wasn't hard.

By the time we finally pushed the herd of cows into the big corral, a bunch of Laura's neighbors were sitting on the fence by the barn, waiting. Laura's branding crew had arrived. She waved and hollered hello to them and then slid off her horse to close the corral gate.

Old Smoke was all lathered up and puffing from running about three times farther than he needed to, just doing things the hard way as usual, but he pawed the ground impatiently, still ready to go.

"Knock it off, you ornery fool," Laura told him, rubbing his sweaty, itchy face affectionately. I noticed she was puffing about as hard as he was. He must have given her quite a ride out there in the brush.

She didn't close the gate after all. She just stood there, holding it halfway open.

"Okay, Dare," she said, "you're riding the cutting horse. Get in there and cut all the cows out."

I gave her a blank stare. "Me? I don't know nothin' about cuttin' cows out. You do it."

Laura laughed and gave Smoke a friendly slap on his neck. "Not on this baby," she said. "Ol' Smokin' Joe's had about all the cow education his feeble brain can handle today. He's got himself so steamed up he'd be more likely to take the cows over the gate than through it." Ty had just come trotting up on Chance but Laura intercepted my glance in his direction.

"And Chance isn't trained for cutting yet, either," she said. "So it's up to you and the Chief."

Oh, no, I wasn't about to go out there and try to do something I didn't even understand. Out of the corner of my eye I could see that the branding crew had all moved over where they could get a better look at what was going on here. They'd get a real charge out of watching Laura's pet delinquent make a fool of himself.

I held Chief's reins out to Laura. "You can take him," I said.

Laura didn't take him. Instead she pushed back her hat and gave me a scornful look. "What's the matter, Dare? Scared you can't handle it?"

She was doing it again. Jerking me around by playing on my pride. I knew it but I still rose to the bait. I could feel my temper and my face start to burn as I turned and swung into the saddle.

"No, Laura," I threw over my shoulder. "I ain't scared of nothin'." Considering my performance at the Calgary jail, it had to be my biggest lie yet. Laura ignored it.

"All right," she said, "the object of the exercise is to get rid of the cows and keep the calves in. Pick yourself a handy cow, show her to the Chief and then just hang on, he'll do the rest. If you change your mind and want to let a cow go, just lay your hand on his neck. That tells the horse to quit and wait for new orders. Go ahead, I'll watch the gate for you." She turned and walked away.

I looked at the milling herd of cattle. Pick a cow, Laura had said. Okay, you there, with the long horns, you're it. So much for step one. Now, show her to the Chief. Hey, uh, listen up here, Chief. You see this big, ugly, mean-looking cow over here? Chief just stood there, half asleep.

Laura was waiting by the open gate. "Come on, Dare," she hollered. "Let's do it today, okay?"

Chief woke up and tossed his head up and down a couple of times like he was seconding the motion. "Sure, Laura," I yelled back. "I'm startin' right now."

"Go get 'em, kid," a voice from the top-rail audience boomed. I glanced over. It was Jim Walker, Laura's next-door neighbor. He and his wife, Mary, had stopped by a couple of times since Tyler and I had been here. I guess he was just being friendly but I didn't answer. I wasn't feeling friendly. I was just feeling stupid out here with everybody looking at me.

All right, Chief, you know-it-all horse, go ahead, do your stuff. Make me look good for a change. I nudged him toward the long-horned cow. Instantly, his ears flattened, his neck stretched out and, like greased mercury, he slid between that cow and the rest of the herd. I couldn't believe it. In one split second a Mack truck had turned into a Ferrari.

The cow slammed on the brakes. So did the Chief.

164

They stood there, face to face, eyeballing each other like a couple of gunfighters waiting to see who would make the first move. The cow broke first. I couldn't believe thirteen hundred pounds of ugly fat could move that fast. In a split second she had pivoted and swung back the other way. The Chief was still with her — and I was still with him, hanging on for all I was worth.

Suddenly the cow gave up and turned and trotted obediently out the gate, the Chief and me right behind her. Everybody on the fence cheered. I turned red and quickly picked another cow.

This one was even faster than the last one. She bolted across the corral but we were right there when she stopped, still face to face.

"Nice work!" somebody hollered from the fence and I turned to see who it was. At that exact moment the cow dived in the opposite direction. So did the Chief. Right out from under me.

The ground was soft and all that got hurt was my dignity. I sat up slowly and spat out a mouthful of cow-flavored corral dirt.

About six people were standing around staring down at me. Laura was one of them. At first I thought she was actually worried about me. Then I saw the grin she wasn't even trying to hide.

"It ain't funny," I spluttered.

"Told you to hang on," Laura said. "Well, don't just sit there. You've got cows to cut. Gonna let Chief do it all by himself?" I followed her gaze just in time to see the Chief trotting that cow out the gate on his own. I groaned. Even the horse was smarter then me. But I got back on and tried again.

Half an hour later the cows were all cut out and, although I'd never have admitted it, I'd had a pretty good time with the old Chief.

Then we got to the hard part. Laura and Ty started heeling calves — Laura had brought in a different horse and Chance seemed to be working pretty good for Ty — and the rest of us worked in two teams on the ground. Jim and Mary and I were together and Laura was heeling for us.

She brought in the first calf. "Okay, Dare," Jim said, "you hold this leg right here, like this." It wasn't as easy as it looked. The calf was some upset. And he was about to get more upset. I learned right then that this whole deal wasn't any fun for the calf. In fact, it was a downright dirty business, but Jim and Mary worked so fast I figured most of it was over before the calf really knew what was happening.

In about two minutes that calf had been vaccinated, ear tagged and castrated. Then Jim reached for the first branding iron — there were three of them. LM with a running bar, a straight line after the letters, was Laura's brand.

He laid the hot iron against the calf's hide. I heard the sizzle of burning hair and skin and a cloud of stinking yellow smoke billowed up into my face. And all of a sudden, right there in the hot July sun, I went ice-cold inside. I could feel the cold, hard knot begin to spread outward from the core of my guts and I swallowed hard. The sounds of the bawling cattle, the yelling, laughing crew, were suddenly faint and far away. The hot, dust-hazed corral was moving away, getting dim and distant.

But I was the one who had moved. Eight years in one second. Back to the last time I'd smelled burning skin. Back to the fire.

I let go of the calf's leg. "Hey, kid, wake up." I heard Jim's voice from somewhere, maybe close by, maybe a hundred miles away. "Hang onto him! We're not done yet."

Oh, yeah, I was done. I couldn't handle any more of this. Slowly, my mind still eight years away, I stood up. The calf scrambled free and landed a well-aimed kick on my shin as he did, but I barely felt it. I had to get out of here.

Laura was shaking out her rope, getting ready for another calf. She glanced in my direction, stopped what she was doing and stared at me.

"Dare!" she yelled over the bawling of the cattle. "What do you think . . ."

I didn't hear the rest. I was running across the corral. Out of the corner of my eye, I saw her turn her horse in my direction. I could hear more shouts, feel the curious looks burning into my back as, one by one, the whole branding crew focused in on me, watching this weird kid freak out.

"Dare!" Laura's voice was closer. I didn't look back. I just kept running. Then I saw Chief tied to the outside of the corral where I'd left him. I don't remember climbing the six-rail fence, but the next thing I knew I was swinging into the saddle and turning Chief down the trail. He must have sensed the wildness in me because he took off at a dead run. We cleared the creek in one giant leap and just kept on running the whole mile to the west fence. I had to stop then to open the gate.

That cooled me down a little. I couldn't just keep running forever. I had to stop and think. I knew where I was going to go. To the big spring. Ty had shown it to me once. It was near here and it was a real quiet place. Somewhere to get my head together. Chief was pretty well winded so I just led him.

The spring was in a thick patch of spruce and it formed a big basin where water came up out of the ground with so much force that bubbles were always rising to the surface of the pool, making it look like a volcano or something.

I tied up the Chief and then just sat there staring into the water trying to think — and trying not to think, too, I guess. I don't know how long I was there. I didn't have my watch but it was a long time. The sun slid behind the tops of the big spruces and cool shadows spread out but I still didn't move. There was no place to go.

I couldn't go back. I could see them all sitting around Laura's big kitchen table, laughing and talking. Probably talking about how that crazy Jamieson kid freaked out this afternoon. Maybe they were right. Maybe I was a little crazy.

Dusk was settling in when suddenly Chief threw

up his head and gave a loud, excited whinny. I knew what that meant. Another horse was coming. But I didn't even look up. There were only two possibilities of who could be coming looking for me and I didn't want to see either one of them.

A horse's legs passed by. Black-stockinged legs, blending into silver blue. Smoke's legs. Laura. I still didn't look up. A dusty, manure-stained boot stepped down. Another one. The boots came closer. The silence grew. Well, come on, Laura, say it. Go ahead, rag at me for being useless and unreliable and a lousy cowboy to boot. I don't care what you say. Just don't stand there with that accusing look I know you've got on your face.

Finally Laura's voice broke the silence. "Could have picked a place with less mosquitoes," she said, pulling up a chunk of log and sitting down beside me.

I gave up and looked at her. "I suppose you think I owe you an explanation."

Laura sighed. "No, Dare, you don't owe me anything. But you owe something to yourself, and I think you better settle the account pretty soon or you won't be able to afford the interest. Whatever you're keeping locked inside you is tearing you apart and you know it."

Yeah, Laura, I thought. You're more right than you know. It's driving me crazy. But that doesn't mean I can talk about it.

I turned away from her and went back to staring into the water. Laura stood up.

"Well, come on," she said tiredly. "You can't sit here all night."

We rode home together but neither of us said another word.

Ty was in bed so I undressed without turning on the light, hoping he wouldn't wake up. I didn't need one of his twenty-questions conversations tonight. I eased into bed, making sure the springs didn't creak, and reached for the blanket.

"Dare? You okay?" Ty's voice came out of the dark.

"Yeah. Sure I'm okay. Just go to sleep, will ya?"

I lay still a long time, listening to him breathe, not daring to move in case he decided I was still awake and ready to talk. I was getting a cramp in my leg.

"Dare?"

"What?" I said through my teeth.

"What happened this afternoon?"

"I don't want to talk about it."

"It's got something to do with what happened to Mom, hasn't it?"

An alarm went off in my head. I sat up. "What are you talking about? You were too little. You don't remember . . ."

"Yeah," he said softly, "I remember, sort of — "

I cut him off. "Well, let it go at that, kid. Don't try to remember anymore." I swallowed. "Just trust me, Ty. You don't want to know. And I don't want to talk about it. Not now, not ever."

170

There was a long silence. "You talk about it in your sleep, Dare."

I went cold. "What?" I whispered.

"You always have. Ever since Mom died."

"What do I say?"

"Nothing that makes sense. Just somethin' like, 'No, Mom. It should have been me.' "

I buried my head in my pillow. I was right. It should have been me.

I didn't go to sleep for a long time. I was scared to. I knew that when I did, I was going to dream about it again.

I did.

171

Chapter 21

I came awake with a jerk as something heavy landed on my chest. It was morning and Ty was standing over me with a mischievous grin on his face.

"Happy Birthday, Dare," he said. "Wake up and open your present."

I lay there blinking and slowly absorbing what Ty had said. July tenth, the date on my watch read. Yeah, it really was my birthday. I was sixteen. Old enough to drive Keith's bike legal now. If he ever let me drive it again, which I doubted. All my life I'd wanted to be sixteen, and now, with everything that had happened, I'd almost missed the big day.

I sat up, tore the wrapping off my present and then just stared at it. A hunting knife. The knife I'd been wanting for years. And wanting was as far as I'd ever got. The price tag on those things ran at about forty bucks. "Hey, where'd you get the money for this?" I asked suspiciously.

"Not polite to ask," he said innocently, but I already knew the answer. There was only one place he could have got it. From Laura. Just great. That meant he would have told Laura why he wanted it. And now she'd make a big fuss about it being my birthday and . . .

"Don't you like it?" Ty's puzzled voice interrupted my thoughts. I looked up at him guiltily and grinned. Good old Ty, he never gave up. No matter how bad I treated him he still hung in there just wanting me to be the Lone Ranger so he could be Tonto.

" 'Course I like it, dipstick. Why else would I have been passing out hints about it for the last five days?"

I was wrong about Laura. She didn't make a big fuss about my birthday. She didn't say a word about it at breakfast. In fact she didn't say much to me at all. I wasn't too surprised, after what I'd pulled yesterday.

It turned out to be a real hot day for early July. Hot and humid. After all the excitement of the last couple of days, things had slowed down a lot and nobody was doing much of anything. By mid-afternoon Tyler and I and Storm were flaked out on the shady side of the deck. Ty was reading, of course, and the dog and I were trying to catch up on some sleep. Until Laura came out, that is.

"Okay, guys, rise and shine, I've got a job for you." I just looked at her. Even Ty wasn't quite as eager as usual. "You know that little ten-acre field out by the old log cabin on the lease?" Tyler nodded. "Okay. Well, there should be half a dozen yearling steers in there. Go and get them and bring them through the gate into the next quarter where the grass is better."

Now that had to be the most useless job for a hot afternoon that she'd thought of yet. Reluctantly, I sat up straight. "Today?"

Laura gave me a disgusted look. "No, Dare. Yesterday would be fine. Of course I mean today. Why, you too busy or something?"

I glared back at her. "Well, it's about ninety above out there and it's three miles up to that pasture and — "

"Then you'd better hurry up and get started earning your keep," Laura said briskly. Which was a pretty clear way to remind me that, among other things, I owed her twenty-five bucks worth of work.

Half an hour later Tyler and I were pushing our reluctant horses up the trail to the grazing lease. Suddenly I reined Chief in. "Hang on, Ty. I've got an idea."

I'd noticed the other trail before when we were out here fencing. It ran straight west to a closed wire gate with a "No Trespassing" sign on it. Through the gate was a wooden bridge across the creek. A cabin sat off to the north on the edge of the trees. Laura had said that the place was owned by weekend people. Well this was only Tuesday — and what they didn't know wouldn't hurt them. Riding across their bridge was going to be a whole lot faster than riding the three extra miles around to the shallow crossing upstream and back to where the cattle were.

"Come on," I told Ty, "let's do this the easy way."

He looked doubtful. "But Laura said — "

"Laura says a lot of things and you believe 'em all," I said, giving him a scornful look over my shoulder. "You know, Ty, you're turnin' into a real wimp since Laura got hold of you." It was a calculated insult. And it wasn't true, either. But I figured it would work. It almost didn't.

He started to argue. "But what if . . ."

Just then a deerfly took a big chunk out of my shoulder. Furiously, I swatted it — and lashed out at Ty at the same time.

"Look, Ty, you do it your way. If you're so scared of Laura, *you* spend the rest of the afternoon ridin' around the long way in the hot sun. Me, I'm gonna get there, get this stupid job done and have time for a nice cool swim."

Without waiting for an answer, I kicked the Chief into a gallop and headed for the gate. By the time I got off to open it, Ty was right behind me. Silently, he followed me through and waited while I shut the gate and got back on. He was mad at me but I didn't much care. I knew how he wanted things to be. Him and me and Laura. One big happy family. Well, it wasn't going to be that way. So he'd just have to make his choice.

I booted Chief into a lazy lope down the trail but, naturally, on Chance Ty passed me like I wasn't even moving. Then, once he'd got his bit of grandstanding in, he pulled her down to a walk and rode up to the bridge just ahead of me.

Chance picked her way daintily through the weeds along the edge of the bridge but she stopped short when it came to actually stepping up onto the plank floor.

"Come on, girl," Ty said softly, "it's just an old bridge. It won't hurt you. You've been over the one at home lots of times." He nudged her with his heels and firmly reined her straight ahead. But no dice. All of a sudden she gave a panicky snort and whirled around on her hind legs.

Typical, I thought. That horse was nothing but a spoiled brat. Ty might have the patience to ride her, all right, but I figured what she needed was a good kick in the ribs.

Now he had her turned around and was trying again. "Easy, Chance . . ." Two steps forward. "Atta girl." Three steps back.

Okay, that about did it. "Just get that brainless nag outta my way," I said. "Chief'll go across." The old clown might not be long on class but he wasn't stupid.

Ty gave me a resentful look but he didn't argue as he reined Chance in behind Chief.

I walked the big horse up to the edge of the bridge. Without hesitating he stepped up onto the first plank. It echoed hollowly under his steel shoe. His ears shot forward and he jerked his foot back to solid ground.

I nudged him with my heel. "Come on, Chief, get up there," I ordered. Obediently, he stepped forward, put one foot on the bridge and balked again. He bent his neck, put his nose down real close to the planks and blew suspiciously. I could feel Ty watching me, not saying a thing but thinking plenty. Thinking that I wasn't doing such a great job of getting across this bridge, either. There was a difference, though, I thought, feeling the anger rising in me. My horse wasn't going to get away with it.

In one fast motion I gathered up the ends of my reins and slapped Chief on the rump with them — hard. At the same instant, I jabbed my heels into his ribs. He threw his head up and gave a startled jump. Then he stepped up onto the bridge with both front feet. That's more like it, I thought. Raising his feet high like he was walking through thistles, and snorting nervously, he took another step. And another.

I gave Ty a triumphant glance over my shoulder. "See, told you he'd do it. Come on, make Chance follow. There's nothin' to — "

I heard the splintering sound and felt Chief's front quarters go out from under me in the same instant. I grabbed for the saddle horn but it was too late. Turned around in the saddle like that, I was already off balance, and the jolt of Chief going down was all it took to throw me over his head. It all happened fast, but even before I crashed onto the floor of the bridge in front of him I knew what had happened — and why it happened. The planks were rotten and Chief had broken through.

I lay there for a second, stunned, wondering if I was unconscious. It seemed so dark, like something was blotting out the sky. Then I knew what it was. Chief's huge body was swaying above me as he reared and pawed at the air, desperately trying to get back on solid footing. But more planks kept breaking. Even above the sound of the horse's terrified snorts I could hear the sound of cracking wood.

Suddenly my numbed reflexes came to life and I tried to roll away from those thrashing hoofs. But it was too late. A crushing weight landed on my chest and that was it. I couldn't move. I couldn't even breathe. A red haze started to roll across my brain like a bank of early-morning fog, threatening to wrap me up and carry me away somewhere. Shaking my head, I fought it off. I wasn't going to pass out.

Far away, I could hear more crashing, and then the weight was gone. I could breathe again — sort of. My brain shook itself out of the haze and started yelling orders at my body. Come on, stupid, get up! What're you gonna do? Just lay there and wait for the horse to land on you again?

Okay, okay, I'm trying. Awkwardly, I managed to scramble to my feet just in time to see Chief turn and half jump, half fall off the edge of the bridge. There was a loud splash as he hit the water, and then silence.

Still half stunned, I staggered a couple of steps and then stood, swaying, as this huge wave of pain and shock and dizziness swept over me. I looked down. I was standing at the very edge of what was left of the bridge floor. I tried to take a step backward, lost my balance and saw that cold, dark water coming up at me.

Chapter 22

The shock of hitting the water brought me back to full consciousness real fast and my first reflex action was to gasp for air. I gulped a lungful of water instead, went under and sank like a rock. The water couldn't have been all that deep. Ten, maybe twelve feet at the most, but it felt to me like I was headed for a closer look at the *Titanic*. I seemed to go down forever and when I finally did hit bottom it was a soft, oozy mud bottom that seemed to reach out for me, trying to grab me and hold me under until . . .

Panicking, I kicked free — and at the same time stirred up a cloud of silt so thick I couldn't even tell which way was up. It was something I'd have to decide on real soon.

Instinctively, I started clawing my way toward the surface, I hoped. I was running short of time — and air.

My head broke the surface and the dazzle of the afternoon sun almost blinded me. I sucked in air gratefully. Then, treading water, I shook my hair out of my eyes and looked around.

What was left of the bridge was behind me but I couldn't see the Chief. He was probably halfway home by now, I thought sourly, looking over at the bank just in time to see Ty pile off Chance, throw her reins over a willow branch and come charging toward the water. I'd better get out of here. The next thing I knew he'd be jumping in to save me or something.

A halfhearted dog paddle was the best I could come up with but it was only a few yards to shore anyway. I felt my feet touch bottom and I stumbled the rest of the way through the shallow water.

I staggered up onto the muddy bank and flopped down, too tired to move. Just lying there being able to breathe seemed like a real accomplishment.

"Dare! Are you all right?" Ty was shaking my shoulder and yelling in my ear at full volume.

"Yeah, yeah, I'm all right," I croaked. I sat up, tried to take a deep breath and started to cough. That's when somebody stuck a butcher knife in my chest. At least that's what it felt like. Half scared of what I'd see, I raised my head and took a look. No knife. Not even any blood. But my shirt was torn open and there on the side of my chest, already turning an awesome shade of purple green, was an almost perfect horseshoe print. I groaned. Whoever said horseshoes were good luck needed his head examined.

I ran my hand over the bruise cautiously, and wished I hadn't. Something in there was messed up pretty good. Busted ribs most likely. Maybe just cracked, if I was lucky. Well, they wouldn't kill me, and even if they did, at least it would be faster than lying in the mud here giving blood donations to a few thousand mosquitoes. Slowly, holding my ribs with my hand, I stood up — and swore as another stab of pain lanced through me.

Ty was staring at me with big, worried eyes. "Dare," he began, "are you sure you're — "

"I said I'm okay!" I snarled, feeling a flash of red-hot fury go through me. "Just leave me alone and help find that idiot horse. He's probably halfway home already and I don't feel like walkin'."

"Chief's right over there," Ty said, looking past my shoulder.

I turned around and breathed a sigh of relief. For once the Chief hadn't taken advantage of the situation. He was standing on the creek bank about fifty yards downstream, looking like a drowned rat and acting kind of subdued for a change. He hadn't even come over to keep Chance company.

I walked over to him. My wet jeans clung to me and water squelched in my boots with every step. He raised his head when I got close but he still didn't move.

"Come on," I muttered, picking up the muddy reins and starting to lead him away. He didn't follow.

"You stupid horse," I said, giving the reins a jerk that probably hurt me more than it did him. Angrily, I looked back over my shoulder, and for the first time I noticed the way Chief was standing. The tall swamp grass along the beaver dam almost hid it, but now, looking closer, I saw that he was putting all his weight on three legs. The left front one was bleeding and he was holding it up so the hoof just brushed the ground. There was something weird about the way the leg was bent.

And then it hit me. Oh, no, I thought, rubbing my hand across my eyes. This is all I need.

"Hey, come on, Dare. Let's go home," Ty was already on Chance and trotting toward me. Suddenly he reined in. "Dare? What are you waiting for? Can't you get on? Hey, you really are hurt, aren't you?" He started to get off.

"Stay on the horse," I ordered. "I'm all right but you better get Laura. Tell her I think Chief's leg is broke."

Ty's eyes left mine and his gaze moved down Chief's leg. I could see the color drain out of his face. He looked up. "But if it's broke he'll have to be . . ." He couldn't finish the sentence. I was glad.

"Come on, Ty, grow up. It's just a horse. Now quit starin' at me and do what I told you. Hurry up. I ain't got all day."

He didn't stop staring. For what seemed like forever those accusing eyes stayed on me. I glared back at him. But for the first time I could remember, I was the one who looked down first.

That broke the spell. Without another word, Ty slammed his heels into Chance's ribs, spun her around on her hind legs and took off down the trail at a dead gallop.

For a minute I could hear the fading echo of Chance's hoofbeats. Then nothing but the faint trickle of water running over the edge of the beaver dam and the steady hum of hungry mosquitoes. It was just the two of us. Me and a horse that didn't know he was going to die.

I turned to look at him. He was standing quiet, calm, his long black tail patiently switching mosquitoes. Once in a while he'd lower his head and blow through his nostrils like he was worried about something, but that was all. Outside of that and the way he was holding that leg you'd never know there was anything wrong with him. Except for the puzzled way he kept looking at me. Like he expected me to do something. I don't know. Maybe I was just imagining that part.

By now I was starting to come down with a pretty good case of guilt and I wasn't handling it very well. I'd gone through so much of it when I was seven years old that it was like having a disease real bad. I'd been immune to feeling it much ever since. Until now.

When it came right down to it, the horse was handling this whole mess better than I was. As I stood watching him, he shifted his weight a little and I realized that the least I could do was to get that heavy saddle off his back.

It took me three tries to heave it off him and when I finally did the pain in my chest just about knocked me out. But I didn't care. Maybe that was one way to start paying. I leaned my face against his neck and waited for the world to quit doing cartwheels. Chief turned his head around and gently nibbled my shoulder. I looked up at the big, honest white-starred face. You stupid horse, I thought. I did this to you. The least you could do is hate me. And now you want to be friends. I swallowed hard and reached up to rub the side of his face, squashing a dozen mosquitoes that had settled there. Then I rubbed my bloody hand across my stinging eyes. Hurry up, Laura, I begged silently as I put my arm around Chief's neck. He leaned his nose against my shoulder and we stood there, waiting.

At last I heard the distant sound of a motor. Thank God. I couldn't take much more of this. Nothing could be as bad as the waiting. At least, that's what I thought until Laura and Ty got out of the truck — and I saw that Laura was carrying a rifle. Then I knew I'd been wrong. This *was* going to get worse.

Laura's face was like granite and she looked ten years older than when we'd ridden away this afternoon. She wouldn't even look at me. She just walked up to the Chief and held out her hand to him.

"Hey, old fella," she said softly, "it's okay. Look, I brought you something." She opened her hand and Chief's nose reached out and his ears went forward. Carefully, he accepted the sugar from her hand and crunched it down. Laura bent and looked at the leg. She didn't touch it. Just looked, gave the horse a pat on the neck and reached down for the gun she had laid on the ground.

I'd known all along it was going to happen. From the minute I'd seen the leg, I'd known. But when she reached into her pocket, brought out the shells and started loading the gun, that suddenly made it real.

Chief finished the sugar, turned and looked at Laura and whinnied softly. Wanting more? Or just wanting Laura not to leave him? Suddenly it struck me how long she'd had that horse. He was eighteen years old. Older than I was. And she'd raised him from a colt. Eighteen years of being Laura's horse.

I made myself look at her. "I'll do it," I said, wondering even as I said it if I really could. I held out my hand for the rifle.

Laura turned toward me. Her eyes were ice. "No, Dare. You've done enough. The only thing this horse has left is a chance to die decently. This is one job you're not going to mess up."

For the first time in my life, I didn't fight back. I just stood there while she tore me down and I took it. Laura reached for the bridle reins.

"Just get out of here, Dare," she said, her voice so quiet it was dangerous.

I hesitated. All of this was my fault. I couldn't just walk away.

Laura's eyes flashed. "You heard me. Go. Get out of my sight." Her voice was shaking now.

I started to turn away but I stopped. Just for a second, I laid my hand on Chief's neck again. It felt warm and silky, full of power. Alive.

I started walking. I could hear Chief start to

crunch one more lump of sugar. I kept walking —
and waiting. A hundred yards. Do it, Laura. For
God's sake get it over with. Two hundred yards.

The shot shattered the air and I jumped as if it
were me that bullet had torn into but I didn't look
back. I broke into a run. With every step the jolt
sent a wave of pain through me. I was glad. It gave
me something to keep my mind on. Physical pain is
the easy kind.

I couldn't stop running. I wanted to. My body
was finished but my mind wouldn't let it slow down.
Not until I was home — that was the second time
I'd thought that word about Laura's place — and
fell face down into the clover-scented grass of the
backyard.

I don't know how long I lay there with my breath
coming in gut-tearing sobs that drowned out everything else. Except for what was going through my
mind. Nothing could drown that out. The same
thoughts just kept repeating, echoing through my
head like a stuck record. This time you've really
done it, Dare. This is the worst you've messed up
since . . .

Stop it, I wanted to scream. Leave me alone.
Don't you ever quit? Don't I ever get to forget?

Chapter 23

I groaned and turned over on my back — just in time to get a face full of big, wet tongue. It was Storm, her eyebrows crooked with concern, licking my face and doing her best to give me doggy-breath mouth-to-mouth resuscitation. And, bad as I felt right then, there was something about that big, smelly dog grin of hers that I couldn't resist. I started to laugh — and stopped again real fast when I found out how much it hurt. I sat up and hugged her, and just holding her warm, comforting body made me feel a little better. Until I remembered how warm Chief had felt the last time I touched him.

I pushed the dog away and slowly stood up. I walked up the back steps of the house. Just the screen door was closed. Inside, the kitchen was warm and clean and full of sunshine. I went in. A familiar smell came to meet me. It was weird. It seemed like a smell I was supposed to like but right now it almost turned my stomach. Dazed, I just stood there in the middle of the floor trying to think of what to do next.

I turned to glance down the hall — and froze as I caught a glimpse of someone standing down there. Then I took a second look. Oh, man, was I spaced. That was me I was staring at, reflected in the long mirror at the far end of the hall. But it didn't look much like me. My hair was hanging in my eyes, curly like always when it gets wet, but stiff in the places where it was caked with mud. My eyes looked funny, glassy, like I was high on something, and so dark they seemed more black than blue. There was a big raw patch on my cheekbone where I'd hit the rough planks on the bridge, and even through the tan the rest of my face was white. I looked for all the world like I was going to be sick. All of a sudden, I realized why that was. I *was* going to be sick.

I made it to the bathroom and sank down by the toilet just in time. I threw up until it felt like my insides were in shreds and all that was holding me together were my arms wrapped around my chest. But at last it was over. I reached up weakly and flushed the toilet and then sank back into a heap on the floor, thinking I was going to die — and hoping it would be soon. Finally, though, the pain in my chest eased back to a steady throb and I started to feel a little better. Better enough to notice that I'd left a muddy trail all the way from the back door and that the bathroom floor looked like a wet dog had been rolling on it.

I dragged myself up on the edge of the tub, sat down and tried to pull off my boots. No deal. They'd dried just enough to begin to shrink and they might as well have been welded to my feet. Somehow, though, I managed to pull my mud-caked jeans off over the boots. I threw them and what was left of my shirt into the tub and headed for the kitchen. The hall mirror threw my reflection back at me again. I shook my head. Calvin Kleins and cowboy boots. Pretty sexy stuff, man. Could start a whole new trend.

I managed to pry the boots off with the bootjack Laura kept by the back door but, as I turned around, those muddy tracks on the floor caught my eye again. Okay, okay, Laura, quit haunting me. I get the message. Wearily, I opened the broom closet and dragged out the mop. See, Laura, I thought, working my way down the hall, you really are getting me broke. A month ago I wouldn't have done this.

Sure, Dare — it was that sarcastic voice in my head again — you've come a long way, baby. You don't mess up Laura's house anymore. Now you just kill her horses.

I threw the mop in the corner. Stop thinking, Dare. Do something, anything. Just don't think.

I grabbed some clean clothes out of the bedroom and headed for the shower. I'd heard of people drowning their sorrows. The way I was feeling, maybe I'd just drown myself.

I stayed in the shower for a long time, soaking

in the comfort of the hot water, trying to ease some of the pain away. I guess it helped some but I ran out of hot water before I ran out of pain. And no amount of hot water was going to do anything for the big, hollow, guilty ache inside of me. Nothing could touch that. It was too deep — and it just kept getting worse.

I got dressed and stretched out on my bed feeling so lousy I just wanted to go to sleep for about a million years. I couldn't do it, though. Not even for a few minutes, 'cause I couldn't quit thinking. Finally, I gave up and wandered back to the kitchen. I looked at the clock above the sink. Nearly eight. Laura and Ty had been out there for over two hours. What were they doing, anyway? It doesn't take that long to kill a horse, does it, Dare? a voice inside me asked, skillfully twisting the knife in my guts.

Leave me alone! I didn't mean to do it.

The rich, spicy smell I'd noticed when I first came in still hung heavy in the kitchen. Suddenly, I recognized it. Lasagna. I glanced at the oven control. It was still turned on. Laura must have forgotten it when Ty came tearing in to get her. I turned the oven off but I didn't look inside. The way my stomach felt I couldn't handle the sight of food. Not even lasagna, and that's saying something. I could eat that stuff three times a day for a month and never get tired of it. And Laura had never once made it since we got here. Too complicated, she always said.

So why now, Laura? Why on a hot, muggy, July day did you decide to stay in the house and cook when you could have been out chasing cows? If you'd have been with us . . .

I turned away and started for the door. And then I noticed something else. Sitting on the counter was one of those big, circular tins, the kind Gram always used for carrying cakes to bake sales and stuff. I lifted the lid.

The cake was huge. A three-decker devil's food — she sure got that part right, I thought grimly — with chocolate icing, white writing and sixteen red candles. HAPPY BIRTHDAY DARE, it said.

And then, all of a sudden I understood everything. That whole big deal about how Tyler and I just had to go move those cows this afternoon. It had all been a setup. She just wanted me out of there so she could do all this.

A wave of sickness that wasn't physical swept through me. No, Laura. You can't do this to me. Not now. So far it's been even between us. War. A fair fight. I hurt you, you hurt me. Well, today was real even, I thought, trying to swallow the bitterness that was threatening to choke me. You made me a birthday party and I killed your horse. Happy birthday, sweet sixteen. Oh, yeah, birthdays were just great. The two worst days of my life had been birthdays.

I wanted to cry. I just wanted to lean my face against the cupboard and bawl like a baby. But I couldn't do it. I knew it would hurt too much. I swallowed the sob that was rising in my throat and wiped my hand across my eyes. For one more second I just stood there, staring at the cake.

"I hate you, Laura!" I yelled at the empty kitchen. I slammed my fist against the counter and then turned and plunged blindly out the back door.

The air was heavy and time seemed to hang suspended like the milling clouds of mosquitoes that gathered in the humid evening. Everything felt like it was waiting. Waiting for something to happen. Something *was* going to happen, all right. Laura was going to come home and I would have to face her. And that was something I knew I couldn't do. Running time again, Dare.

I went back inside and got out the duffel bag again. Most of the stuff I'd put in there last time was still there. It was enough. When you don't know where you're going, you travel light.

A few minutes later, I was outside again, standing on the step with the bag beside me. *Now* what was I waiting for? Wherever I went, it was going to be a long walk. I'd better get started. If I stood around here much longer Laura and Ty would show up and I could say good-bye in person. Yeah, that would be great. Good-bye, Laura, it's been a blast. Thanks for the birthday party, oh, yeah, and sorry I killed your horse.

And Ty? Just a few hours ago I'd been wishing he'd make up his mind. Laura or me? Well, from the way he'd looked at me back at the bridge, I knew he'd finally made his choice — and it wasn't me. I was free to go. So why didn't I?

Slowly, I started walking across the yard. And that's when it finally hit me — the thought that had been hanging around the fringes of my mind for a while now, trying to sneak out whenever I let my guard down. I didn't *want* to go. Not anymore. I didn't know how it had happened or when it had happened but somehow this place had started to feel like home.

Great time to notice it, Dare, I thought bitterly. Now that it's too late. Now that you *can't* stay here any longer. I knew it was true. I'd blown it. After what I'd done, Laura wouldn't be able to stand the sight of me — and I wasn't so sure that I'd blame her.

Still, I didn't move. I just stood there, looking. Noticing things in a whole different way, now that I wasn't going to be seeing them any more. Everything was so green and quiet and peaceful. Everything looked right, like it belonged here. Storm, knotting her eyebrows with concentration as she gnawed another huge bone into white sawdust, the saddle horses grazing down by the creek.

I noticed that Chance had been unsaddled and turned loose with the others. That figured. However upset he was, Ty would always do the right thing, look after his horse first. That was my brother for you. About as different from me as he could get. A funny feeling ran through me as I thought that and, in that second, I couldn't decide if what I was feeling for my brother was admiration or hate.

It wasn't something I wanted to find out and I was glad when an impatient whinny from the corral caught my attention. Smoke, of course. The whole rest of the world could be enjoying a peaceful summer evening but he was restless, as usual. I watched him trotting back and forth along the corral fence, tossing his head. Now and then he stopped, pawed the ground and gave another loud, defiant whinny. I knew what part of his problem was. He was hungry. Laura always fed him at five and his supper was way overdue. I sighed. Okay, Smoke, one last time. On account of I owe somebody around here something.

I headed for the bale stack to get him some hay. But just as I was about to drop it over the fence for him I thought of something else. There was no shelter in that corral and if it looked like a storm Laura always put him in the barn at night. Well, from the way those thunderclouds were building in the west, it looked like a storm to me. I sighed and carried the hay into the barn. I brought Smoke's halter back out with me. The stallion watched me come into the corral. He snorted and took a couple of steps backward, nodding his head up and down playfully. Horse, this is no time to play games with me, I thought, feeling my temper start to glow.

"Whoa, Smoke," I ordered, walking toward him. This time he held his ground, watching me. That was more like it. I reached up to put the halter on him. He'd never seemed so tall before. Oh God, my side hurt. I gritted my teeth as I fastened the snap on the halter. Oh well, things could have been worse. At least Smoke hadn't given me any real trouble —

With the speed of a striking snake the stallion cut that thought off in midair as his head shot forward and, with a loud *thunk*, his big, yellow front teeth took a patch of cloth out of my shirt sleeve.

That was close — too close. "Quit it, Smoke!" I yelled, giving the halter a painful jerk — painful for me, I mean. Either that move impressed the horse or else he was satisfied that he'd made his point. He gave me his gee-whiz-what-are-you-so-mad-about-I-was-only-kidding look and followed me meekly into the barn. I put him in his stall, fed him and closed the barn door for the night.

Chapter 24

I was just picking up my duffel bag again when I heard the truck drive up. Well, now I'd done it. Hung around till it was too late to run. Well, I'd still go. I'd just tell Laura I was leaving. It would be the only good thing that had happened to her all day.

I stood on the step and waited. Laura and Ty got out of the truck and walked silently toward me. I guess I was about half spaced anyhow, but the whole scene had kind of an unreal quality to it. I felt like I was watching it on a movie screen. The slow, stiff way they moved, the mud-smeared clothes, the drained look on their faces made me think of the way the convicts always looked at the end of a hard day in one of those chain-gang movies. And their hands. Blistered so bad they were almost bleeding.

All of a sudden it made sense. Why they'd been gone so long. Yeah, killing a horse is fast. But burying one isn't. The thought didn't make me feel any better.

Ty walked past me into the house. He wouldn't even look at me. But Laura gave me a long look — and her eyes were so cold a shiver ran through me. I saw her gaze take in the duffel bag on my shoulder and then slowly come to rest on my face. Waiting for me to say something.

She'd have to wait a long time because there was nothing left to say. Except maybe, "I'm sorry." And for once in my life I really did want to say it. But I knew I couldn't. I was already too close to the edge. Too close to falling apart right there in front of her. And I couldn't take the chance. Not after all those years of building up a wall of toughness I'd be safe behind. It's just like I read once about why oysters make pearls. They get a grain of sand in their shell and it keeps rubbing on that one spot until they can't stand it any more so they cover it with this stuff to make it quit hurting. Finally all the layers of stuff turn into a pearl. I guess I'd been doing the same thing ever since Mom died. Building up layers of protection.

Now all my defenses went on red alert and I lifted my head and met Laura's eyes with a cold stare of my own. Our eyes held for a long time. Laura finally broke the silence.

"Where do you think you're going?" she asked, her voice as bleak as her eyes.

I shrugged. "I don't know," I said, my voice cool with practiced arrogance. "Anywhere. As long as it's away from here. Why? What's it to you?"

I couldn't read the expression that crossed

Laura's face. At first, I almost thought I saw regret. But then that look was gone and I understood the one that replaced it all too well. Contempt.

"You tough kids are really something," Laura said in a voice that cut. "You destroy everything you get close to and then when the going gets rough, you run." Her eyes sliced across me and then, like I wasn't even there, she pushed past me and reached for the door handle.

She was close enough that I could have touched her but I still yelled the words at her.

"Yeah, Laura, that's right, I'm runnin'. What do you care? You never wanted me. You wanted Ty and got stuck with me as part of the package. One big, stupid hood thrown in free. Well, your problems are all solved. Ty won't follow me now. You've got him. And I'm gone. Doesn't that make your day, lady?"

My voice was starting to crack and I finally shut up. Not waiting for an answer, I turned to go, throwing the duffel bag over my shoulder as I turned. That movement sent a jolt of pain tearing through my ribs. I caught my breath and, without thinking, pressed my hand against my side. And of course, Laura noticed. I knew by now there wasn't much that Laura *didn't* notice.

"What's wrong with you?" she asked gruffly.

I dropped my hand and straightened up. "Nothin'," I shot back defiantly.

I wasn't sure Laura bought it. The look she gave me wasn't exactly convinced. But then she sighed.

"All right, Dare." Her voice was as soft as it was bitter. "Go — and solve all your problems, and mine. I won't try to stop you. But — " she gave me a long, thoughtful look like she was still trying to decide about something " — wait until morning and I'll drive you to town. Then you'll be on your own. From the looks of you, you aren't in any shape to start walking tonight."

Yeah, I added silently as she opened the door and went in, and from the looks of you, you aren't in any shape to drive me tonight. Reluctantly, I followed her inside. Now that I'd made up my mind to go, I just wanted to do it, to go before leaving got any harder. I had to admit Laura was right, though. The only place I felt like going now was to bed.

Laura threw her jacket over a chair. "Supper's in the oven," she said. "Help yourselves. I'm going to bed."

"I'm not hungry," Ty muttered. I didn't say anything. Laura was already gone anyway.

That left just me and Ty. We stood there across the room from each other, both pretending the other wasn't there. It was a weird feeling. I'd been with him ever since he was born. I knew him better than I knew myself, understood what he was thinking, could predict his next move before he even figured it out for himself. So why did he seem like a stranger now?

Finally we quit playing games. We looked at each

other. And that's when I understood. My kid brother wasn't there anymore. When he raised his eyes to meet mine the innocence was gone. His eyes were hard now. It was the first time that I realized he really *did* look a little bit like me.

"You wanna know something, Dare?" he said at last, in a voice that came out real soft — so soft it was scary.

No, I didn't want to know. I just stood there, wishing he wouldn't tell me.

But he told me. His eyes never wavered and his voice stayed just as calm. Maybe that's what made it so hard to take. Slowly, each word dropping into the silence of the room like a pebble falling into a deep hole, he said it.

"That horse you killed was a better person than you are, Dare." He stood there, staring at me, waiting. Waiting for what? For me to yell at him? Hit him? For what? Telling the truth? I didn't do anything. "You wanna know something else?" he burst out, the calmness gone. "I hate you!"

He spun around and ran down the hall. I heard the door of our bedroom slam behind him. I sank down in a chair and laid my head on the table. You're not the only one, Ty, I thought, feeling the tiredness spreading through me like liquid lead. I just wanted to be asleep.

The next time I looked up it was dark outside. My watch read eleven forty-five. I'd been asleep all right — for over three hours. I dragged myself to my feet. Oh, man, did I feel lousy. Ty must be sleeping by now and all I wanted to do was lie down. I headed for the bedroom.

It was pitch dark in there so I didn't bother getting undressed. I just pulled off my sneakers and lay on top of the covers. It was too hot for blankets anyhow. Gradually, as my eyes adjusted to the darkness, I could see Ty lying there. His bed was between mine and the window so the faint light from the yard light on the barn touched his face. He looked like himself again when he was asleep, I thought.

I eased over onto my good side and tried to relax. It didn't work. My muscles felt like they were in knots and just breathing hurt enough to keep me wide awake. And besides that, I couldn't stop thinking.

I don't know how much time passed. At night, time gets all messed up. Seconds turn into hours on you. I do know I was awake for a long time, though. I listened to a lonely coyote howling his heart out down in the woods somewhere and wondered what he'd do if he never got an answer. I listened to a few stray cars crunching gravel as they passed the gateway and wondered where they were going — and where I was going.

Then there was another sound, closer. Ty tossing restlessly in bed. So he wasn't asleep any more, either. I wondered what he was thinking — but if it was about me I didn't want to know.

Hey, come on, Dare. What's the big deal? Your

kid brother grew up and doesn't need you any more. He finally found out you're not a hero after all. So you're free. Tomorrow you're getting out of this dump. Alone. How's it feel to be free, Dare?

I jammed my fist into my pillow. Shut up. Shut up and leave me alone. I don't want to think.

I drifted into a feverish half sleep but another sound woke me up. It was so low I could barely hear it but it was real close. Muffled sobs. Ty must have his face buried in his pillow, trying to keep me from hearing. He had that kind of pride. And he didn't cry easy. Poor kid must be pretty tore up, I thought, automatically starting to ease myself out of bed. I'd promised I'd be there when he needed me.

But then I realized what I was doing and sank back against the pillow. Forget it, Dare. This time he *doesn't* need you. This time it's *you* that made him cry. How could getting what you'd thought you wanted hurt so much? I wondered. I swallowed hard and turned my face into the pillow. Go ahead and cry, kid, I don't blame you. And, while you're at it, cry a little for me, too.

Gradually the sobs grew fainter and the room was quiet again but I couldn't sleep. I was still awake when the first distant rumble of thunder sounded in the west. At last. The storm that had been waiting to happen all day was on its way. I could see the flicker of lightning across the sky. The wind was coming up. I could feel it coming through the open window and touching my hot face with its cool fingers. It was going to be quite a storm. Well, let it storm. Let it crash and bash and break things. Let it do all the things I wanted to do. I lay there feeling the tension in me build with the storm.

The first real close crash of thunder was almost a relief. Like it was smashing a hole in the sky to let the pressure off. Come on storm, go for it. Blow the lid off.

And that's exactly what it did. I'd never seen a thunderstorm like it. It seemed like it just sat there, right overhead, and went through its whole bag of tricks — rain, wind, even a little hail, but mostly thunder and lightning, almost continuous and so close you couldn't spit between the flash and the crash. I guess it was kind of scary but I liked storms and they never scared me.

The room lit up daylight bright and, in the same instant, the whole house seemed to explode, leaping and shuddering with the deafening crash that echoed through it. Without knowing I'd moved, I found myself sitting bolt upright in bed, shaking. Everything was dark again and I could feel the hair on the back of my neck standing on end. That had been *so* close.

"Dare!" Ty's voice was high with terror. "Dare! Where are you?"

I was out of bed then. "I'm here, Ty," I said, my voice coming out calmer than I thought it would. "It's okay."

The next thing I knew Ty was hurling himself into my arms with the force of a runaway train. The jolt in my ribs almost knocked me out but I didn't care. Having Ty's arms around me made up for a lot of pain. I could feel him shaking, his heart pounding against my chest.

"Hey," I said, holding him tight. "Take it easy, huh? We're okay. It didn't hit us."

"Well it sure as heck hit something." Ty's voice was still shaky but I could feel him beginning to relax.

"No kiddin'," I said, letting go of him and reaching over to flick the light on. I wasn't surprised when nothing happened. "Power's off. Let's go see if it hit the transfomer pole."

"Okay," Ty said. I turned away to look for my sneakers but he stopped me. "Dare?"

"Yeah?"

He swallowed, hesitated, and I could feel his eyes on me. Then, "Dare, I — didn't mean what I said tonight."

"Forget it. I had it comin'."

"No, Dare — " he began.

I opened the door. "You comin' with me or you gonna stand around and talk half the night like usual?"

"I'm comin'," he replied instantly.

Laura was already in the kitchen when we stumbled in. She had a flashlight in one hand and was dialing the phone with the other. When she heard us she shone the light in our direction. "You okay?" she asked.

"Sure, Laura," Ty said. I didn't answer. I didn't

figure it had been me she was asking anyway.

"Hello?" Laura said into the phone. "This is Laura McConnell and . . . No! I don't want to listen for the beep and leave a message. I want my electricity back. Tonight. Isn't there anyone alive down at that . . ."

I shook my head in the darkness. Good old Laura. Still trying to make the world run according to the rules. Her rules. Just like she'd tried to do with me. Won't work, Laura. Haven't you learned yet?

Suddenly there was a crash of shattering glass and I jumped. Dimly I could see Tyler over by the sink. He'd been getting a drink and dropped the glass. Now he was staring out the window.

Laura jumped, too. She hung up the phone and turned toward him. "Tyler, what on earth . . ."

Suddenly he came alive. "The barn," he said, in a voice that sent a chill up my spine. My eyes followed his gaze out the window, and then I understood.

Flames, Day-Glo bright against the black sky, were leaping from the barn roof.

"Oh my God," Laura said, barely above a whisper. "So that's what it hit." Even as she said it she was reaching for the phone. "Afraid it's already too late for the fire department," she said as she began to dial. "But," she added with a sigh of relief, "at least none of the horses are in there tonight."

Chapter 25

A physical shock tore through me so hard I felt my knees go weak. I went cold all over. This couldn't be happening. Even I couldn't have done it. Laura's two favorite horses in one day.

"No!" I screamed into the darkness of the kitchen. Then I was running for the door.

"Dare, what — " Laura began but then she was back on the phone line. "Yes, I've got a fire! My barn. Laura McConnell. Four miles west and — "

The slamming of the door behind me cut off the rest. I just kept running toward the barn. Until the solid wall of heat hit me, that is. I stopped about fifty yards in front and stood, half blinded by the brightness of the flaming roof.

Nobody could go into that burning hell. And for me, just being this close to a fire was hell. I started to back away. But as I did, I heard Laura's words again. "You destroy everything you get close to." Right on, Laura. First Chief. Now Smoke. But you don't know the half of it, Laura. And you don't want to know. *I* don't want to know.

But I couldn't stop remembering. The fire brought it all back, clearer than ever. In those few seconds there in front of the barn I relived it all. I was seven years old all over again. Seven and scared out of my mind by what I'd done. And it all started out so innocent, that day in Vancouver.

That's where we lived. In two rooms on the second floor of an old house on the wrong side of Vancouver. I guess we were pretty poor. I never knew it then, though. There was always enough to eat and we knew Mom loved us. It never occurred to me that there should be any more.

Mom was a waitress and her shift didn't end till four and then she had to pick Tyler up at day-care so I was usually on my own for about half an hour. That was okay. I was proud of being trusted with my own key and everything. It made me feel real grown up. Until the day I found out the hard way that I was still just a little kid.

It was February 14. Mom's birthday. She always made a big deal out of us kids' birthdays. Well, this time it was my turn to do something real special on her birthday. And I did. Oh God, did I ever.

At the Valentine party at school that day the teacher gave us each a big, gooey cupcake with red cinnamon hearts in the icing. The minute I saw mine, I knew I wasn't going to eat it. I was going to save it.

I managed to get it home in one piece — sort of. It got a little mushed on one side when I dropped my lunch box, but I pushed it back into shape a little when I got home and it was perfect. I got the birthday candles out of the drawer and then I climbed up on the counter to get the matches off the top shelf. Mom kept them way up there on purpose. Us kids weren't supposed to touch them. Not ever. But that day was special.

I planted one red candle in the middle of the cupcake and looked it over. Not enough. Maybe one in the middle and four in a circle around it. That looked better. I would have put even more on but I was running out of space and the edges were getting crumbly.

I looked at the clock. Ten past four. Show time! I took out one match and closed the box carefully before I struck it. Then, concentrating hard, I held the flame to a candle. One lit. Two. Three. The match was getting short. Four. Five. The flame bit my fingers and I threw the burning match stub into the sink and turned on the tap — and Mom didn't think I was old enough to handle fire. I'd done all right, hadn't I? I thought proudly. That match was dead out. Everything was safe.

I glanced out the window. Sure enough, Mom's old Volkswagen Beetle was just turning into our street. Right on time. Carefully, holding my breath so I didn't jar the candles, I picked up the birthday cake and carried it to the window. The car stopped and Mom got out. Just like always, she looked up at the window to see if I was there. That was what

I'd been waiting for. Holding the cake in both hands, I lifted it as high as I could reach. I wanted to be sure she could see.

That was when the first candle fell off. I saw it start to go, the overloaded top of the cupcake crumbling, the candle leaning a little farther. I made a grab for it — and knocked another one over. Hot wax splashed on my other hand and, without thinking, I let go. The cake hit the counter and smashed into a dozen pieces. Candles flew in all directions. One bounced against the curtain. Like a sudden burst of fireworks the thin material blossomed into golden flame. Desperately, I grabbed for it. If I could pull it down, throw it in the sink like I had the match . . .

But all of a sudden, my shirt sleeve was magically disappearing in a burst of flame, too. I tried to get rid of the curtain but it was sticking to me, melting onto me like some monster from a horror movie.

Panicking, almost too scared to feel the pain, I grabbed a chunk of the sticky, burning cloth in my hand and threw it as far away from me as I could. It landed on yesterday's newspaper, lying beside the garbage can. It started to burn, too. I was surrounded by fire. My clothes were burning. My hair was burning. Everything blurred into a nightmare of flame and pain and suddenly I knew I was going to die. I started to scream for Mom.

She came. The door burst open and she was running toward me, coming through the flames, reaching out to me. I can remember her wrapping her arms around me, smothering the flames against her body, picking me up, holding me. The sound of sirens outside. Breaking glass. Mom lifting me through a burning window frame. Strong arms. Cool air. Being carried down a ladder. And somewhere, a woman screaming . . .

I woke up in a hospital room. The doctor said I was real lucky. Except for a couple of scars on my neck that I keep my hair long enough to cover, I came out without any permanent damage. Physically, anyhow.

Right after Mom handed me out the window, the ceiling collapsed. She was pinned under it. They couldn't get her out in time.

I shook my head, trying to make the memory go away. This was the worst it had ever been. It was so real I could still hear Mom screaming. But then I realized the screaming *was* real. It was Smoke. I could hear his hoofs crashing against the sides of his stall as he fought to break free. And in between the crashes he just kept screaming in terror. Horses scream a lot like people.

I started to run again. Next thing I knew I was at the barn, dodging wisps of burning hay that kept floating down from the open hayloft door and trying to unlatch the front door.

Suddenly, even over the roar of the flames, I heard Ty's voice. I glanced over my shoulder. He was running toward the barn screaming at me. "No, Dare, don't go in there! You're gonna get killed just like Mom!" The scream turned into something more like a sob, and as I jerked the door open I saw Laura coming after Ty. She was yelling at us both.

"No! Don't, Dare. You can't . . . Tyler, come back here!"

I never would have believed she could move that fast. As the full force of the heat hit Ty he hesitated, and Laura caught him. Now she had both arms wrapped around him, but he was still struggling to get away.

"Let go of me, Laura!" I heard him holler breathlessly. "I gotta stop him." He aimed a purposeful kick at Laura's shin.

I stood there for a second, disoriented in a world of red-tinged blackness where the hot, smoke-saturated air burned my eyes and bit my lungs. Coughing, I started to feel my way down the aisle between the stalls. Smoke's stall was the last one. He was still screaming and kicking but even that was almost drowned out by the terrible sound of the fire as it roared hungrily through the hay-filled loft above us. As long as it stayed above us we had a chance. Once it broke through the boards of the ceiling . . .

I shouldn't have thought that because, just then, right on cue, there was a cracking sound and a flaming board came spiraling down. It landed in the straw in an empty stall and instantly the straw went up in flames. The fire was downstairs.

At least now I could see where I was going. The firelight cast an eerie reddish glow over everything. Including Smoke. Silhouetted against the flames, he reared again and again and lashed out at the planks of his stall, his hard front hoofs sending splinters of wood flying. His eyes shone red with a satanic glow and even his sweat-soaked silver hide reflected a reddish gleam. He wasn't Smoke anymore. He was a fire-crazed demon horse, a part of this nightmare world we were in.

I knew now I couldn't do it. No one could do anything with a horse gone crazy like that. If I went near him he'd kill me. Another burning board fell. Time was running out.

I looked behind me. There was still a pathway to the door. If I got out now . . . "Sorry, Smoke," I gasped between coughs. I turned away, took a step and stopped. "And when the going gets rough you run." The words echoed through my head.

I grabbed Smoke's halter rope from the nail on the wall. He had his halter on.

"Whoa, Smoke!" I yelled at him above the roar of the flames. He stood still a second, trembling. I unlatched the gate. He reared again, his hoofs flailing the air above my head. I stood my ground. "Stop it, Smoke! Stand still!" His hoofs crashed to the ground, missing me by inches. I took a step forward and, in one fast motion, snapped the rope into the halter ring.

A board fell across the aisle. Smoke recoiled against the back wall of the stall, snorting with terror. I pulled on the rope. "Come on, Smoke," I yelled hoarsely. "We gotta get out of here." But it was no use. To get out of the stall I had to make him come right *toward* this latest patch of flame. I looked at his terror-glazed eyes and knew he'd die before he'd do it. We both would.

It was his eyes that gave me the idea. Something I'd seen in a movie once. A blindfold. That's how you were supposed to get horses out of a fire. You covered their eyes so they couldn't see the flames and then they settled down and trusted the hand on their halter. Oh, yeah? I figured Smoke trusted me about as far as he could throw me — which might be quite a ways in his case. But anything was worth a try. I peeled off my shirt and, dodging the panicky nip he aimed at my shoulder, quickly wrapped the shirt around his face and tied the sleeves together under his jaw.

"Okay, Smoke, it can't hurt you now, come on." I pulled on the halter rope, and he reared back, almost jerking me off my feet. I swore at the pain that tore through my side but I didn't let go. Stupid horse. Hadn't he seen the movie? I was shaking now — as much from anger as fear. I jerked the rope. "Quit it!" I yelled. Smoke stood still for a few seconds, trembling and uncertain, and I cooled down a little. I reached out my free hand and gently touched his face. "It's okay, I'm still here. I'm gonna get you out of this."

Then, slowly, his black velvet nose reached out toward me. I could feel his warm hay-scented breath as he sniffed my face. I took a short step back, not even tightening the halter rope. Smoke took a step, too, staying close enough to keep his nose against my shoulder. We were both still shaking.

There was fire on all sides now. I had to pick my way between the patches of burning straw. Once I had to step right through the flames — but Smoke kept coming. I really thought we were going to make it. Then, without warning, a chunk of blazing board came plummeting down from directly above us. It hit Smoke's rump and bounced off so fast I doubt it even really burned him. But he gave a squeal of terror and lunged sideways, slamming me against the tack-room door. I heard myself scream as a huge wave of pain engulfed me. Everything started fading away. I couldn't breathe. My knees started to buckle.

Then suddenly something jerked me back to consciousness. That smell. The same burnt-flesh smell that had freaked me out at the branding. I felt a sickening pain in my shoulder and instinctively jerked it away from the door, but it wasn't until I caught a glimpse of the long red welt on my skin that I realized it had been *me* that had been burning. The door's metal latch was red hot. There was a lot of fire behind that door. When it broke through . . .

No! I wasn't going to die like that. Not with just a few feet left to go. "Come on, Smoke." I locked my fingers into the noseband of the halter and stumbled toward the door.

It wasn't till the rain hit my face that I knew. We'd made it. We were outside. Laura and Ty were still there. She was still holding onto him. He was still screaming at her. Nothing had changed. I couldn't understand it. Why hadn't anything changed? I'd been in there for hours. For a lifetime.

Suddenly, Laura looked up — and froze. She looked like she was seeing a ghost. Come on, Laura, shape up, will ya, lady? Come and get your stupid horse. I'm too tired to hold him anymore.

Now she was coming toward me. Running in slow motion like she was in a TV commercial. I held out the rope. "Here," I managed to croak. And then she didn't even take the rope. She just let it drop. Come on, Laura, I went to a lot of trouble to get that horse. I could feel myself swaying, like a tree that was getting ready to fall.

Laura's arms were reaching out toward me. She was saying something. She sounded mad, as usual. I tuned in to some of it. ". . . you crazy, pigheaded, wonderful . . ." It wasn't till her arms closed around me that I realized it was me she was talking to, not the horse. Her timing wasn't bad. She caught me just as the world started to go real funny, red fire and black sky, rotating like the pinwheel Mom had bought me at the fair a long time ago.

Mom. Hey, Mom. I did better this time, didn't I?

Tyler's voice was penetrating the whirling darkness. I knew what he was saying.

"Are you okay, Dare?" It seemed like he was always saying that. Sure, I was okay. I was the

Lone Ranger — and he was Tonto. And Laura? Laura would always be Laura. Tough old Laura. Always there to catch you when you needed her.

I needed her now. There were some things I had to tell her.

point

Other books you will enjoy, about real kids like you!